ARIZONA GOLD

ARIZONA GOLD

by

Dean Ashton

Dales Large Print Books
Long Preston, North Yorkshire,
BD23 4ND, England.

British Library Cataloguing in Publication Data.

Ashton, Dean
 Arizona gold.

A catalogue record of this book is
available from the British Library

ISBN   978-1-84262-817-1 pbk

First published in Great Britain in 1963 by Robert Hale Limited

Copyright © Jim Bowden 1963

Cover illustration © Stephen Carroll by arrangement with
Arcangel Images

The moral right of the author has been asserted

Published in Large Print 2011 by arrangement with
Mr W. D. Spence

Dales Large Print is an imprint of Library Magna Books Ltd.

Printed and bound in Great Britain by
T.J. (International) Ltd., Cornwall, PL28 8RW

ONE

The horse, its colour hidden by the dust of long travel, dragged its hoofs over the parched ground. Its head sagged dejectedly and the weary animal could not make the effort to swish the flies away with its tail.

The reins, which hung loosely round the horse's neck, had long since slipped from the rider's fingers allowing the animal to find its own way without a guiding hand. The dust of distance disguised the man's torn, travel-stained clothes. He sat motionless in the saddle, his head slumped on his chest. A battered, wide-brimmed sombrero clung precariously to his head affording some relief from the merciless beating of the sun which had sapped the energy of both man and horse.

The cowboy's mind had almost ceased to function reasonably. His eyes, stung by the dust and sand, and hurt by the scorching sun, had stopped searching for a water-hole. They closed in their effort to cut out the shimmering, dancing glare from the desert.

The miles dragged painfully. Night would bring some relief but even the darkness could not banish the tormenting thirst.

Something stirred within the cowboy. His hand reached for his water-bottle and raised it to his swollen lips but no trickle touched the broken skin. He looked at it stupidly; his eyes focused on the bullet-hole which had deprived him of his only water. The bottle slipped slowly from his grasp and fell to the ground to lay, evidence of his passage as horse and rider moved wearily onwards.

The horse dragged up a short rise, its movement getting slower as it neared the top. A few minutes passed before the rider realised that the animal had stopped. He raised his head and squinted through burning eyes at the undulating bareness which stretched ahead broken only by outcrops of barren, grey rocks and prickly cacti. The cowboy slipped and half fell from the saddle. He dragged himself to his feet and patted the horse's neck.

'Sorry, old fella,' he croaked. 'Guess you jest can't carry me further; but we've got to keep goin'.'

He staggered forward and the horse, relieved of its burden, followed slowly. The heat from the ground burned through the cowboy's worn riding-boots. His heart throbbed; his brain pounded and fear filled his eyes. He glanced furtively behind him and tried to hasten his step. He stumbled and turned; his eyes narrowed, searching the waste he was crossing.

'They're coming!' he mumbled. 'Coming! Coming!'

He dragged himself forward, glancing frequently behind; expecting to see some shadow on the trail, some hand reaching out for him. How many times he fell only to stagger to his feet; how far he travelled stumbling, crawling, the cowboy never knew but the sun was still glaring fiercely when he staggered up a rise to the rim of a hollow.

'Water!' The word pounded through the jumble in his brain. He stared with un-believing but hopeful eyes. His sombrero fell from his head and rolled grotesquely down the slope. The man's knees buckled; he swayed on the edge of the hollow and fell forward, rolling over and over, faster and faster down the dusty slope to the bottom where the last turn left him prostrate, his arms outflung, his face to the burning sky.

The faithful horse followed its master slowly to the hard bowl. It muzzled the cracks beside the still form searching in vain the ground which had once held water.

When the lowering sun sent a black shadow from the rim of the hollow to envelop the prone cowboy he stirred. His eyes opened painfully and stared at the blue sky fired by the setting sun. He turned his head slowly, his eyes seeking relief in the shadow. Suddenly he started. Two figures walked towards him! He struggled to roll over but the effort was too great and he fell back. Saved! Saved! The word pounded in his brain. He turned his head again to see his saviours but his eyes widened with horror.

'Not you!' he croaked, his cracked swollen lips trembling with every word. 'No! Not you!'

Fear dragged some hidden strength from the tortured body. He rolled over, struggled to his knees and pushed himself to his feet. He staggered around in an attempt to run but after half a dozen paces fell to the ground. Frightened sobs racked his body as he rolled on to his back. With a great effort he raised his head and recoiled in horror as the two men, their faces laughing grotesquely at him, walked nearer and nearer. He shrank from them as with every step they grew bigger and bigger.

'Shoot me! Shoot me! Finish me!' The

words sounded like thunder in his mind but were in fact only a croak from his throat.

He struggled to sit up propping himself on his left elbow. His right hand searched frantically for his Colt and in his frenzy he found some lost energy. He jerked the gun from its holster and pointed it waveringly at the two faces looming above him. He squeezed the trigger six times drowning the frightened whinny of his horse. He squeezed again but as the hammer clicked ominously he saw the faces were still laughing at him.

In the utter, desperate exhaustion of finality he sank back to the ground.

TWO

'Grandpa, it's time you came in.' The soft voice interrupted Manuel Cordoba's thoughts as he rocked contentedly in his chair on the veranda of his house.

In spite of his eighty years Manuel loved to sit outside and watch the changing colours as night spread from the edge of the desert across his beloved valley.

'Let me stay a little longer, Conchita,'

Manuel's gentle voice mellowed with years of happiness, whispered persuasively. 'Fetch your wrap, my child, and sit with your grandfather for a little while.'

Conchita flashed a warm smile at Manuel and hurried into the house. A few moments later she returned, laid a thick woollen shawl around her grandfather's shoulder, swung a delicately worked wrap round her own and sat down at the old man's feet.

Manuel smiled and laid a hand on her shoulder. 'Thank you, my dear,' he said. His eyes shone brightly as he gazed at his grand-daughter following the flow of her thick black hair over her shoulders. He admired the smooth, olive skin of her face and the beau-tiful clear-cut features but most of all he loved her eyes, deep set, arched by thin, black eyebrows; brown eyes which he knew could flash with a quick fiery temper but which could change suddenly with a soft, loving tenderness. Manuel rocked and sighed for his youth.

Conchita loved her grandfather deeply, more so since her father and mother had died and her brother had married. Although the managing of the ranch had been handed over to her brother, Carlos, Manuel remained head of the household and was consulted on many decisions. Manuel had been pleased when his great grandson had been born for it meant that a Cordoba would continue to run El Rancho Sierra de Espuma. But, now, Manuel wondered if this would ever come about; how long could he keep the serious situation from his grandchildren? His outward contentedness hid an ever present worry which he always hoped might vanish without Conchita and Carlos knowing.

Manuel and his granddaughter shared the silence as night fell across Cordoba Valley and lights came on in peon's huts. Suddenly the quietness was broken by the scurry of sandals across the hard ground.

'Pedro, what is it?' asked Manuel as a short swarthy peon reached the foot of the veranda steps.

'*Señor Manuel,*' panted the Mexican, 'Josef Gonzales returns.'

Manuel sat upright, his body alert. 'Josef? But he should be riding the western perimeter.'

'*Si, señor,*' answered Pedro. 'But he returns with a Yanki.'

The old man sprang from his chair, his eighty years a lie to his activeness. 'A Yanki! Go, Pedro, quick; tell Josef to come straight here.'

The Mexican scuttled away and as the clop of horses' hoofs came closer Conchita rose to stand beside her grandfather.

'Who can it be?' she asked.

'We shall see,' replied Manuel. 'He must have come off the desert for Josef to find him.'

As the figures emerged from the darkness Conchita gasped and clutched her grandfather's arm when she realised that the bundle thrown across the saddle of the weary looking horse was a man.

Josef Gonzales, tall in the saddle, halted the two horses in front of the veranda, swung lightly to the ground and threw the reins to Pedro who ran alongside. Before Josef could speak Manuel was alive to the situation. He issued orders quickly and precisely.

'Conchita, tell Maria to bring some hot water to the guest bedroom quickly. Pedro, help Josef to carry the man inside.'

Manuel led the way into the house and they were met at the bedroom by Maria, the fat, motherly housekeeper to the Cordoba family, who immediately took charge of the situation. When she was satisfied that she could manage with only Pedro's help she bustled everyone else from the room.

'Where did you find him?' queried Manuel

as he and Josef strolled back on to the veranda.

'In a dried-up water-hole,' replied Josef. 'I was riding the western perimeter on the edge of the desert when I heard six rapid shots. I could see nothing, *señor*, but rode to investigate and I found the Yanki, an empty gun beside him, his horse a few yards away.'

'And that is all?' asked Manuel.

'*Si, señor*,' replied Josef, 'nothing else. I don't know why he had fired, maybe a last effort to attract attention.'

Manuel stroked his chin thoughtfully. 'He looked as if he'd been a long time in the desert,' he murmured.

Josef nodded. 'His tracks came from the desert's heart.'

'Then God help him,' whispered Manuel. 'He must have suffered.' He looked hard at Josef. 'You have done well. You may as well stay in the bunkhouse for the night and return to your patrolling tomorrow.'

'Very well, *señor*,' answered Josef. He strode down the steps and led the two horses to the stables.

Conchita, who moved closer to her grandfather and took hold of his arm to go inside, shivered.

'What is the matter?' asked her grandfather. 'Are you cold?'

'No,' replied Conchita. 'Let us go inside.'

Manuel held back. 'You can't fool your old grandfather; something's worrying you.'

'It's nothing really,' answered the girl but her voice was far from convincing. When pressed for an explanation Conchita was reluctant to speak. 'It's silly, I suppose,' she said, 'but I feel there's going to be trouble through this man!'

THREE

Conchita stopped sewing and gazed at the man in the bed. He had been unconscious for three days and his face was pale beneath its weather-beaten brownness. Furrows cut deep in his forehead and his cheeks were drawn back but in spite of the effects of his ordeal Conchita could see that he was good-looking in a rugged way and she estimated that he was little more than her own twenty-two years. Conchita turned back to her sewing.

An hour passed when suddenly she started. There was a faint movement beneath the sheets. The girl put down her sewing and crossed quickly to the bedside. Slowly the man's eyes flickered open and for a few moments stared vacantly at the ceiling. Sensing the presence of someone beside him he turned his head slowly and stared at Conchita.

'Where am I?' The whisper was hardly audible.

Conchita leaned forward, smoothed his dark hair back from his brow. 'It's all right,' she said gently. 'You are safe.'

The cowboy sighed deeply and turned his head. He glanced round the room seeing a heavy, dark-oak bedstead with matching furniture in neat, clean surroundings. When he looked back at the girl there was a new light in his eyes. Conchita smiled.

'I'll be back in a moment,' she said and hurried from the room.

When she returned the cowboy saw she was accompanied by an old man, tall and thin, who in spite of his years commanded the respect of authority.

'Ah, my son,' said the old man, 'we are glad to see you have pulled through. You have caused us some anxiety.'

The cowboy felt himself enveloped in the warmth of the smile. *'Gracias, señor,'* he whispered. The door opened again and he saw a handsome, young Mexican accompanied by a girl almost as pretty as the one he had found at his bedside. They were accompanied by a fat woman who smiled broadly and carried a bowl.

'I have brought you some soup,' she said and after the young Mexican had helped him to sit up in bed she handed the bowl to him.

The cowboy drank slowly feeling a new life being driven into him. Everyone watched him patiently and it was not until he had finished that the old man spoke.

'We must introduce ourselves,' he said. 'I am Manuel Cordoba, this is my granddaughter, Conchita, my grandson, Carlos, his wife, Rosita, and our housekeeper, Maria, who runs us all.' The laughter which followed this remark made the sick man feel safe and welcome. 'You are at El Rancho Sierra de Espuma.'

The cowboy smiled at each in turn then, looking at the old man asked, 'How did I get here? How long have I been here?'

'One of my riders, Josef Gonzales, found you in the desert. That was three days ago and you have walked close to death since then. Maria, Conchita and Rosita have constantly watched over you.'

'*Señor,*' replied the cowboy, 'I am deeply grateful for what you have done; forgive me if I have been any trouble.'

'It has been nothing, my boy,' said Manuel.

The cowboy saw everyone staring at him expectantly. 'Forgive me,' he smiled. 'I should have told you my name; Wade O'Hara.'

'Wade O'Hara.' The old man repeated the words slowly as if trying to recall whether he had heard the name before. He smiled and shook his head. 'Why were you in the desert alone?' he asked.

Wade hesitated before he answered. 'I lost my way,' he said. Wanting no more questions until he knew more about his surroundings he sank back on his pillows with a sigh. Cordoba was about to speak but to Wade's relief Maria cut him short.

'No more questions, *Señor* Manuel,' she said. 'The young man's tired. Now, out of the room, all of you. There will be plenty of time for talk later.' Maria bustled the Cordobas from the room and a few moments later followed them.

As the door closed behind her Wade looked slowly round the room and thanked the luck which had delivered him from the desert, brought him to this luxury and to the waking sight of a pretty girl.

Half an hour passed and the door opened slowly. Conchita slipped in quietly, closed the door silently and crossed the room to the foot of the bed. She smiled when she saw Wade was awake.

'I thought you might be asleep,' she said.

Wade smiled. 'I had to keep awake to see you,' he whispered.

Conchita blushed, walked to her chair, picked up her sewing and continued to work without speaking. Wade watched every movement, admiring her slim, young body, the dark hair, the pretty face and long nimble fingers. How long he watched her Wade did not know but suddenly the light was fading outside and he realised he must have been asleep. Conchita saw his movement, put down her sewing and lit a lamp.

'You have had a good sleep,' she said. 'It will have done you good. I will get you something to eat.'

Conchita returned a few minutes later with the food and as Wade enjoyed the light diet she watched him, fascinated by the new light in his steel-blue eyes, and recognising, in spite of his thinness, a rugged, handsome look. She recalled the human bundle she had first seen thrown across the horse but knew now how well he would sit in a saddle. But her thoughts were troubled as she watched his long, supple fingers handle the food and she was reminded of the smooth butt of the Colt which lay with his gun-belt in a drawer. She knew those fingers and that butt could mean only one thing – a gunman; and yet she could see no evil in the young face. She longed to ask him questions but her grandfather had forbidden it saying, 'He will tell us in his own time, Conchita, no man is able to keep his life a secret all the time.'

When Wade had finished his meal he suddenly asked, 'Was I alone when I was found?'

Startled by the suddenness of the question Conchita hesitated and Wade looked at her curiously. 'Yes,' she answered. 'Only your horse was with you. Should there have been someone else?'

'No; only I seem to remember someone.' Wade paused trying to recall his last memory in the desert. 'I guess the heat made me imagine things.'

'Probably,' agreed Conchita.

'Do you get many callers?' asked Wade. Although the question was put casually Conchita felt it had some connection with what had been said before.

'No,' answered the girl. 'Apart from the

people in our valley you are the first person we have seen for over two months.'

A sense of relief passed over Wade and even Conchita noticed it. She was puzzled.

During the following fortnight the Cordobas spent a lot of time with Wade. They were pleased with his progress but they came no nearer to learning about Wade's past. He felt in some way he was letting them down by shrouding it in mystery but need they know any more about him?

At the end of the second week Wade was allowed out of bed and during the following week Conchita spent a great deal of time helping him walk around the room bringing strength back into his legs. Wade found the pretty face had driven the two hideous countenances from his dreams and he found himself longing for the next day when Conchita, her arms supporting him, would help him round the room. One day they stood gazing through the window at the leaping fountain in the courtyard, sharing each other's silence, when Wade turned Conchita towards him. Her upturned face welcomed him as he gazed into the shining depths of the dark-brown eyes. Slowly their faces came together. Wade kissed her gently; he felt her lips accept him and his right arm encircled her pulling her closer until he felt the fullness of her body. As their lips parted Wade started to apologise for the liberty he had taken with the girl who had befriended him but Conchita stopped him. 'I've longed for you to do it,' she said. Their lips met again and the past and the future no longer mattered to Wade, only the present was important.

Two days later Conchita burst into Wade's room.

'You come to table with us today,' she said excitedly.

Wade's eyes lit up. 'This means I can start getting outside again,' he said.

Conchita nodded. 'Maria says the sun and fresh air will put the finishing touches to your recovery.' Her eyes were alight with happiness and Wade took her hands, pulled her towards him and kissed her.

'Much of that recovery is due to you,' said Wade. 'Thank you, Conchita, for all you have done.'

'It was nothing,' she replied quietly, her eyes suddenly showing a sadness.

Wade noticed it. 'What's the matter?' he asked.

'Now you are nearly well it means you may soon ride away,' she replied.

The thought of leaving had never occurred

to Wade. Enclosed by four walls he had been cut off from the outside world but now the door was open he must take his place amongst people again. Suddenly the past flooded upon him again. His thoughts were interrupted when he realised Conchita was speaking again.

'...and maybe there's no need for you to go away again – ever. Carlos can give you a job and grandfather will use his influence if I ask him.' She rushed to the door. 'I'll ask him now.'

'No, Conchita, no.' Wade stopped her.

The girl spun round; her eyes flashed alarm and disappointment, 'You don't want to stop!' she cried.

'It's not that,' said Wade.

'Maybe some nice American girl waits for her cowboy to return,' snapped Conchita.

Wade smiled. 'There is no one,' he said. 'Only you.' He took Conchita's hands and kissed her. 'It is just that I don't want you to ask him yet; let me get used to being about and then we'll see.'

Conchita smiled. 'I'm sorry,' she said. 'I'll come back for you in ten minutes.'

When the girl returned she found Wade smartly dressed in the clothes which had been laid out in readiness for this day. His blue shirt matched the colour of his eyes and his black trousers were neatly folded into the tops of shining black boots.

'Something's missing,' said Wade. 'I would like my gun-belt.'

'Gun-belt?' Conchita frowned. 'But you won't need that here.'

'Maybe not,' said the cowboy, 'but I don't feel dressed without it. Please may I have it?'

Conchita walked slowly to the chest of drawers and, opening the second one, pulled out the gun-belt and Colt and held them out to Wade without speaking. He did not notice the troubled look in her eyes as he took them and felt an old power surge through his hands. Now he could deal with anything; he could solve any problem. He buckled the belt tightly, making sure the holster hung at the correct height, at the height at which Wade O'Hara could draw his gun with the greatest possible speed. Conchita frowned as she watched him fasten the thong round his thigh and examine his gun. Wade slipped the Colt into its holster and looked at the girl. He smiled. 'I am ready,' he said.

Conchita did not return the smile but turned and walked from the room. The cowboy followed her along a passage and into a large room the centre of which was occupied by a dark oak table set for the mid-day meal. High-backed, heavily carved, matching chairs were set around it and colourful carpets lightened the dark, wooden floor. Manuel Cordoba stood in front of a huge fireplace talking to his grandson whilst Rosita busied herself with some dishes on the sideboard. They all turned to face the door when it opened.

Manuel stepped forward to greet Wade but he froze in his step when he noticed the gun slung to Wade's thigh. He frowned, but remembering he was the host quickly resumed his smiling composure.

'Welcome, my son,' he said, taking Wade's extended hand.

'My thanks to you, *señor*, for all you have done for me and that thanks goes to all your family,' said Wade.

'Come, Wade, the meal is ready; Maria has prepared something special for the occasion.' Manuel moved towards the table and was about to indicate a chair to the cowboy when he noticed Wade making towards a chair on the opposite side of the table. Conchita noticed it too and was about to stop Wade when she saw her grandfather shake his head.

The conversation flowed across the table during the meal but Wade noticed it was of everyday things; not once was Wade O'Hara mentioned. It was as if the Cordobas were waiting for him to raise the subject. He felt embarrassed; he felt he owed some explanation to these kind people and yet...?

Conchita's thoughts troubled her. Why did Wade flaunt all good manners by wearing his gun and choosing his own place at the table? Up to now she had known him only between four walls; could he be different outside? Suddenly she stiffened; startled by the sudden realisation as to why Wade had chosen his own place at the table. She saw that he had his back to a wall and from his position he could see both doors in the room! Only a man who was in danger of his life; a man who was afraid he might be caught with a gun in his back would go to such lengths! Conchita's thoughts ran wild as the meal continued.

When the meal was over Wade looked hard at Manuel.

'*Señor,*' he said quietly, 'I feel I owe you some explanation.' He paused wondering how much to tell them, wondering what they would do if he told them the full story.

Manuel broke the silence. 'My son, it seems to be causing you some embarrassment to tell us the story.' The voice was kind

27

and comforting. 'Do not tell us unless you wish to. What a man has been, what his future is to be is no concern of ours. We accept you as we find you.' The old man paused letting his words sink in. 'Wade, stay here as long as you want; we like what we have seen of you.'

Wade raised his head slowly. He looked round the table at each of the Cordobas. They answered his glance with a smile but he saw Conchita's eyes were dimmed with troubled thought. He rose and walked to Manuel.

'*Señor*, my thanks to you,' he said. 'Maybe some day I'll tell you my story; in the meantime...'

'You get strong and well again,' interposed Manuel with a smile. He looked at his granddaughter. 'Conchita,' he said, 'show *Señor* O'Hara round the ranch.'

Conchita's worries moved into the background as the days passed and she shared Wade's enthusiasm for the open air. The hours spent with each other drew them closer together. Their love for each other expanded beyond the four walls where it had been kindled.

One day they slipped from the saddles

beneath some cottonwoods and lay in the shade. Wade stared at the blue sky and suddenly realised the happiness he felt had banished the horror which had driven him through the desert. Conchita rolled over towards him, propped herself on her elbows and looked into his steel-blue eyes.

'Wade,' she whispered, 'Today, you never looked behind you. Why don't you leave your gun at home? You've never needed it here.'

Startled by the girl's observations Wade looked sharply at her. 'What do you mean?' he frowned.

'Something has worried you ever since you were brought to us. You've expected someone you did not want to see. We've all noticed it but grandfather would not let us speak about it. It's only today that you've stopped glancing behind you when we've been out riding. What is it, Wade? Whom do you expect?'

Wade pushed himself into a sitting-position. He stared at the ground thoughtfully for a moment before looking into the enquiring eyes which watched him.

'Conchita,' he said. 'It looks as if my past has been laid for ever. Will you marry me without knowing about it?'

Startled by the suddenness of the proposal

Conchita gasped. She scrambled quickly to her knees, flung her arms round Wade's neck and gave him her answer with a long passionate kiss. As their lips parted she whispered an almost inaudible 'Yes.' Their lips met again and locked together they sank to the ground.

'Grandfather will be pleased you are going to stay and Carlos will be glad to have you as a partner; we'll fix everything when we get back,' said Conchita eagerly as they rode home in the early evening. 'They are both pleased with the way you work and handle horses and cattle.'

Wade agreed to let her approach her grandfather immediately. He was happy in this Mexican valley.

As they rounded a bend near the ranch-house Wade pulled hard on the reins. Two men were swinging from their horses in front of Manuel Cordoba who sat on the veranda. Wade's eyes narrowed, piercing the distance between himself and the newcomers. Conchita, who had halted beside him, turned to see his forehead creased by a frown and his eyes darkened with annoyance, anger and hate.

'What's the matter?' she gasped, alarm showing in her voice when she saw Wade's hand close round the butt of his Colt.

'It's too late,' hissed Wade. 'I can never escape from my past!'

FOUR

Wade eased his Colt from its holster. Conchita stared in horror and, as he moved his horse forward, she leaned from her saddle, grabbed his reins and forced both animals back out of sight of the house.

'You can't,' she cried desperately. 'You still...'

'I must,' snapped Wade. 'They were bound to catch up with me; I should have known. The only way is to face them.'

'But there are two of them, you won't have a chance,' she said.

'What else can I do?' replied Wade. 'I should have known it wouldn't work out to stay here.'

A new light flashed into Conchita's eyes. 'They need never know you're here,' she explained eagerly.

'But they may know already,' said Wade.

'We'll have to chance that,' replied Conchita. 'I'll ride in and try to warn grandfather not to say anything. You go round the back and tell Maria not to mention you and then keep out of sight.' Wade hesitated. 'Quick, we haven't much time,' urged the girl and pulling her horse round kicked it into a gallop towards the house.

Wade watched her for a moment and realising that there might be a chance of remaining undiscovered he made his way carefully round the house.

One of the newcomers wiped the dust and sweat from his face whilst the other held his hand out to greet Manuel who had risen from his chair. The sound of hoofs pounding the hard ground made the three men turn to face Conchita who pulled the horse to a halt in front of the veranda.

'I've left Josef down the valley; he will be in later,' she said. She saw the surprised look on her grandfather's face for he knew that she had been with Wade. The two men turned to Manuel and when they did so Conchita flashed a warning with her eyes.

'Very well,' he replied and the girl felt some of the tension ease when she realised her grandfather had understood. He turned his attention to the two men. 'I am Manuel Cordoba,' he said. 'Welcome to my home and please forgive this intrusion. This is my granddaughter, Conchita.'

The two men returned the greeting and removing their dirty, dust-covered sombreros bowed to Conchita. She acknowledged them coolly, unattracted by what she saw. The short, dark cowboy's smile was cold and his brown eyes moved everywhere as if trying to penetrate every corner.

'Glad to know you, miss.' The tall, lean man's voice rasped with a harshness which jarred on Conchita's ears whilst the long scar down his left cheek made her shudder. He continued to speak for them both. 'I'm Jake Saunders an' this is Pete Corby. We've jest come off the desert an' we'd be mighty grateful fer a bunk fer the night.'

'Certainly,' said Manuel, ignoring Conchita's slight shake of the head. 'Pedro!' he shouted and his call was answered by the shuffling of sandled feet. 'Show these men where to sleep tonight,' instructed the Mexican, 'and then see to their horses.'

'Si señor,' answered Pedro.

'Come and dine with us in half an hour,' offered Manuel.

'Thank you,' replied Jake as the two men turned to follow Pedro.

As they walked away Conchita slipped

from the saddle and hurried to her grandfather's side.

'What is wrong, my child; where is Wade?' he asked. 'I gather he did not want to see them.'

'Thank goodness you understood me,' said Conchita. 'They have something to do with Wade's past,' the girl went on. 'They are the reason he wears a gun. He wanted to face them but I persuaded him to keep out of sight until they've gone.'

'He offered no explanation?' questioned Manuel.

The girl shook her head. 'No.' She took her grandfather by the arm. 'We must warn the others not to mention Wade,' she said.

They hurried inside and after explaining the situation to Carlos and his wife they went to the kitchen where they found Wade sitting at the table staring thoughtfully at the Colt in his hand. He looked up when the door opened but relaxed when he saw his friends.

'Conchita has told you about the two men?' he asked.

'What little she could,' replied Manuel testily.

Wade looked uneasy. 'I guess I owe you some explanation,' he said. 'But please wait a little longer and trust me.'

'Just as you wish,' answered Manuel. 'It looks as if your past has caught up with you in the shape of these men.'

'That's right,' said Wade. 'I guess the best thing would be for me to ride out of here and not involve you in my life.'

'Your past would still catch up with you somewhere; why not face it now,' advised the old man.

'The only way I can face it is with this,' answered Wade, tapping his Colt.

'No!' cried Conchita, her eyes filled with anxiety. 'We agreed you would stay out of sight until these men had gone. They need never know you have been here. Carlos and Rosita will not say anything, nor will Maria, and Carlos is out now warning the peons not to say anything about strangers should these two men question them.'

'I don't see why it shouldn't work,' said Manuel. 'Take your meal up to your room and stay out of sight.'

'Very good,' said Wade. 'You are all so kind to me.'

Manuel led Conchita out of the kitchen. 'Don't look so worried, child,' he urged comfortingly. 'You could easily make these men suspicious. Everything will turn out right, I'll see that it does for I see you think a lot of this young man and your happiness means so much to me. I can tell those men are gunmen but they hardly have the stamp of lawmen and yet if they are not why does Wade run away?' The old man looked puzzled.

Half an hour later Jake Saunders and Pete Corby were seated at the table with the Cordobas. Throughout the meal Manuel kept the conversation going on everyday things so that the two men would not notice Conchita's attempt to hide her uneasiness.

When the meal was finished Jake Saunders looked at Manuel. '*Señor* Cordoba,' he said, 'for some time we have been trying to trace a friend of ours, Wade O'Hara; young, about twenty-two, dark hair, blue eyes, rugged but not bad-looking. The last time we heard of him was on the other side of the desert. We wondered if he had crossed and passed this way.'

Manuel looked thoughtful for a moment. 'The name means nothing to me,' he said. 'We get few visitors here and I am sure we would have remembered anyone answering that description, especially Conchita.'

Conchita blushed. Jake Saunders grinned. 'I'm sure she would,' he said. 'Wal, I'm afraid we'll jest hev to go on searchin', Pete.'

Corby nodded. 'I reckon, if *Señor* Cordoba

doesn't mind, we should get some sleep an' make an early start in the morning.'

Manuel rose from his chair. 'By all means gentlemen. Don't let us detain you.'

The two men pushed themselves from the table, bade Cordoba goodnight and left the house. They made their way to the long building in which they had been given a room for the night. As they left the house Carlos moved quickly to the window and watched them.

'They've gone straight to their room,' he reported when he saw a light come on in the room across the way.

'Good,' said Manuel, 'We'll all wait here until Maria has cleared the table. Keep watch, Carlos.'

After the table had been cleared Carlos reported that no one had left the building opposite. 'Now is the time to have Wade down and hear his story,' he added.

'That's exactly what I thought.' Everyone turned round to see Wade standing in the doorway. 'An explanation is needed and now is the time to give it. I too have watched Saunders and Corby settle down. I don't think they will be back tonight but all the same it would be better if someone kept watch.'

Manuel nodded. 'Rosita, you take Carlos' place. Carlos, Wade, come, sit at the table.' The three men sat down; Wade hesitated a moment staring thoughtfully in front of him.

'My story is not going to be a pleasant one,' he started.

Conchita stepped forward suddenly. 'Grandfather, Wade and I...'

'No, Conchita, not now,' Wade interrupted. 'Hear my story first. You may change your mind about me; in fact you may all alter your opinions. But when you have heard me I will stand by whatever decision you make.' He paused, wondering where to begin. Everyone waited expectantly. 'I'm a no-good cowboy,' he blurted out. 'I know no trade except what I can do with this gun.' He patted his holster.

'But you've worked so well round the ranch,' pointed out Carlos.

Wade smiled. 'Oh, I've done a bit of this and that; I've handled cattle and horses but I've never stayed in any job long; I drifted, an' that isn't good for a man. The inevitable happened; I joined up with bad company, the two men who are now asleep over there, Jake Saunders and Pete Corby. We robbed our way across the county but finally I got tired of it and wanted to go straight. They laughed at me and told me it was impossible, once an outlaw always an outlaw, but I was determined to get out because I could see these men hardening and once they started to go for bigger takings there was likely to be killings and I didn't want to be branded a murderer. We had planned a raid on a bank in Colorado but at the last minute I pulled out; this broke the chain with the result Saunders and Corby were caught. They both got three years and they swore revenge when they got out of jail. A year ago I heard they were out and since then it has been a continual problem to keep one jump ahead of them. They caught up with me in Lucero and I figured the only way to outwit them was to cross the desert. Unfortunately they saw me when I tried to ride out at night. One of their bullets hit my water-bottle and I did not find out until it was too late to turn back.' Wade paused. 'Wal, you know the rest. My past has caught up with me again. I don't want to bring trouble to you kind people so I've been thinkin' the best thing to do is to ride out of here tonight.'

'But, Wade,' cried Conchita, 'somewhere they'll meet up with you again; stick to our plan, they'll go away and they'll never look here again.'

'I can see Conchita has some strong feelings about you,' observed Manuel.

'I love him, grandfather,' gasped Conchita. 'It was only this afternoon that Wade asked me to marry him and I said I would.'

'After what I've told you how can you want to marry me,' said Wade dejectedly.

'I care nothing for your past,' replied Conchita. 'I love you as you are.'

Manuel smiled, admiring his granddaughter's trust and deep love. He looked hard at the troubled young man. 'Wade,' he said quietly, 'Conchita expresses all our opinions. I don't think there is any real badness in you; you got off on the wrong foot early in life but at the time when it mattered you decided to go straight. This is a great asset in a man; there are not many who can do that. What we have seen we like and admire; we want you to stay.'

The tension in Wade seemed to flow out of his body. 'Thank you, *señor,* thank you for trusting me,' he whispered.

'Right,' went on Manuel, 'we will keep you out of sight until these men have gone.' Manuel paused. 'Before we retire for the night I think there is something you all should know especially as Conchita wants to marry Wade and that will bring him in as a partner on the ranch.' He paused, looked at Conchita and said, 'Bring us a glass of wine please, my dear.' Carlos and Wade respected his desire for thought whilst the wine was poured. After he had tasted the wine he continued. 'Carlos has some indication of the true position of our affairs but even he does not realise that we are not so well off as it would appear on the surface. I know people think I am still fabulously rich from the gold my brother and I discovered in Arizona.'

'Cordoba!' Wade gasped. 'I knew I had heard the name before; the lost mine of Superstition Mountain!'

Manuel smiled. 'That's right,' he said. 'We bought this valley, made this ranch and helped the peons on our estate. That ran away with a lot of our money. My brother insisted on going back to the mountain but I said we had enough. That was the last I ever heard of him. I used most of the remainder of the money attempting to locate him but it was no use. The droughts over the last two years have hit the ranch pretty hard so altogether we are not in a very good position.'

'Why not use the map again, grandfather, you've still got it,' said Conchita excitedly.

'Let Carlos go.'

Manuel shook his head seriously. 'No,' he said, 'no one of mine will visit that place again. There is nothing but evil there. It has claimed my brother and many others who attempted to find the mine after us. The mountain has a curse upon it.'

'But grandfather...' started Conchita.

'I think the answer lies here,' interrupted Wade. 'I believe this ranch can be pulled round.'

Manuel smiled. 'I'm glad to hear you say that,' he said appreciatively. 'It shows our judgment of you is right. Carlos, Wade will be your new partner in El Rancho Sierra de Espuma.'

Carlos smiled, extended his hand across the table to grip Wade's firmly.

'I think it might be as well if we all went to bed early,' advised Manuel.

Wade rose first bade the Cordobas goodnight. When he reached his room he did not light the lamp but walked across to the window, and stood staring thoughtfully at the light in the building opposite. His thoughts raced across the events of the day and the conversation he had had with the Cordobas. His eyes narrowed when he thought of Saunders and Corby and he wondered if they realised they were so near the map of the fabulous lost mine of Superstition Mountain. He hitched up his gun-belt and adjusted the hang of his Colt before crossing the room to the door where he listened to the Cordobas bidding each other goodnight and going to their rooms.

When he was satisfied that they were settled for the night he gently opened the door and peered along the corridor. All was silence. He stepped out of the room closing the door quietly behind him and moved swiftly but silently along the corridor to the hall where he paused against the front door. No sound broke the stillness and Wade held the door ajar whilst he made sure no one moved outside. Satisfied there was no one about he stepped on to the veranda and stood quietly in the shadows. The light still burned across the way and Wade hurried across the open ground. Reaching the building he inched his way to the window and peered carefully through the glass. Saunders and Corby were sitting on their bunks and Wade noticed that they seemed to be in earnest conversation. He glanced across the room which ran the full width of the building and was pleased to see that the window on the other side of the room was slightly open. He moved quietly round the building until the sound of voices was clearly audible to him.

'I tell you I'm certain,' said Saunders convincingly.

'But you've never seen Cordoba before,' said Corby. 'How can you be certain?'

'The description fits,' replied Saunders impatiently. 'Besides, the name of this place, Sierra de Espuma, the Spanish name given to Superstition Mountain. Only a man who'd had some connection with the mountain would give his ranch a name like thet.'

'Suppose you're right,' said Corby. 'What good will it do us?'

'Numbskull,' snapped Saunders impatiently. 'Do you figure a man would destroy a map of the mine's location? I reckon we could force him to hand it over.'

'Maybe he's kept it in his mind,' answered Corby.

'Use your head,' snapped Saunders. 'If he died suddenly his secret would die with him; he'd want to leave some clue as to the mine's whereabouts fer his family. There must be a map, an' we're gettin' it tonight!'

'What about O'Hara?' queried Corby.

'I ain't fergittin' him,' said Saunders. 'We'll catch up with thet low-down, double-crossin' coyote some day but I don't figure on missin' this opportunity.'

Wade tensed himself; his hand closed round the butt of his Colt. His thoughts raced. He was tempted to reveal himself but realised he could not out-gun both Saunders and Corby. If he called the assistance of Carlos he might only bring trouble to the Cordobas.

Wade moved silently to the corner of the building and hurried to the stables where he quickly saddled his horse. Hurrying back to the ranchhouse he made his way to Manuel Cordoba's room. He paused at the door, pulled his Colt from his holster and stepped swiftly into the room closing the door behind him.

Manuel, who was in bed reading, looked up in astonishment when he saw Wade with a Colt in his hand.

'I'm sorry, *señor*, but things have taken a different turn, I must have that map of the gold mine,' said Wade urgently.

The old man's eyes widened. 'But, Wade after all we've done...'

'It's for your own good,' snapped Wade. 'It would take too long to explain and you probably would treat the matter lightly. It may be too late even now, so quick, the map.'

The door suddenly burst open and Conchita rushed in, tears streaming down her face. 'Wade! Wade! What are you doing?'

Wade gasped as Conchita flung herself at him. He pushed her roughly to one side and she fell sobbing into a chair.

'I saw you go to those two men,' she gasped. 'I thought you said they were your enemies and all the time you have been working your way into our friendship.' Her eyes flashed hatefully. 'We trusted you, I loved you but all the time your only interest was the map.'

'Believe me, Conchita, it's not like that,' said Wade desperately. 'I have no time for explanations.' He eyed Manuel whose face had hardened. 'Thet map, *señor*,' he hissed, 'or else Conchita gets a bullet.' The hammer of his Colt clicked ominously.

Manuel stared wide-eyed at the sobbing Conchita and the cowboy who, only an hour ago, had professed his love for her, but now threatened to kill her for the sake of a gold mine.

'All right,' replied the old man quietly accepting defeat. He swung out of the bed and crossed to the wall where he pushed a picture to one side and pulled out a piece of paper from the cavity in the wall. He held the paper out to Wade. 'There you are,' he said, 'but I'll warn you, it will do you no good. I know that Superstition Mountain will wreak its revenge on you for the work you have done tonight.'

Wade seized the paper without speaking, backed to the door. 'Don't leave this room until I have ridden away or it will bring death to the Cordobas,' he warned. He stepped quickly out of the room and hurried down the corridor. Once out of the house he ran to the stables, seized his horse, jumped into the saddle and left the ranch at a fast gallop.

FIVE

When the door shut behind Wade, Conchita, tears streaming down her face, started after him but her grandfather grabbed her arm and detained her.

'Don't, Conchita,' he said. 'Let him go; we don't want any harm to come to anyone tonight.'

Manuel held his granddaughter as she wept against his shoulder, until the sound of the galloping horse began to fade. The old man pushed the girl gently from him. 'Go and get Carlos,' he said calmly.

Conchita rushed to the door and hurried along the corridor. There was a puzzled look on Manuel's face as he followed her. Conchita pounded on the bedroom door which was flung open by a startled Carlos.

'What's the matter?' he asked when he saw the frightened look of concern on his sister's face.

'The map, Wade forced grandfather to give him the map,' cried Conchita.

Carlos' face darkened. He turned back into the room and reappeared a moment later with a gun-belt.

He fastened it on as he hurried along the corridor. He looked up, startled when his grandfather blocked the way.

'Do not chase him, Carlos,' he said quietly.

'But, grandfather...' started an astonished Carlos.

'It's not worth the risk,' replied Manuel. 'The map will do him no good; there's a curse on that mountain.' He paused a moment looking thoughtful. 'But I think I will save the boy from that fate. Carlos, we can send word north in the morning; our friends will not fail to pick him up and return him here.'

Carlos hesitated. 'Maybe you are right,' he agreed. 'Maybe that's the best way.'

Suddenly the front door burst open and the Cordobas were startled to see Jake Saunders and Pete Corby with Colts in hands run into the house. They had been leaving their room when Wade galloped away from the stable, but they paid little attention to the galloping horse as they hurried across the open ground to the house.

Carlos made to reach for his gun but was halted by a sharp 'Hold it!'

Manuel stepped forward. 'I'm afraid your partner has double-crossed you,' he said. 'I was puzzled when only one horse galloped away but this must be the answer.'

'Partner,' questioned Jake, a frown creasing his forehead. 'We have no partner.'

'Wade O'Hara,' snapped Carlos. 'He's got the map.'

'I thought you didn't know O'Hara,' snarled Saunders.

'We found him in the desert,' answered Manuel. 'We cared for him, and liked him, believed his story but tonight he's shown up in his true colours. The whole thing planned by the three of you but now he's double-crossed you.'

'Sold us out way back,' snapped Corby, hate showing in his eyes, 'but we'll git him; come on Jake.'

Jake remained facing the Cordobas. His face hardened. He moved forward, jerked Carlos' gun from his holster, and brought his own Colt crashing down on the Mexican's head. Carlos fell to the ground without a sound; Rosita screamed and sank on her knees beside her husband. Manuel started forward but Jake threatened him with his gun.

'Thet's so's he can't try to stop us gittin' away,' snarled Saunders. 'An' don't you try it old man.' He spun on his heel and the two men hurried from the house slamming the door behind them.

They ran to the stables. 'Saddle the horses,' shouted Saunders. 'I'll watch the house.'

Pete soon had the animals ready and he led them towards the stable door.

'Everything all right?' he called.

Saunders rose from the shadows and hurried to Pete.

'Shore,' he grinned. 'We hev them scared.' He took the reins of his horse and the two men led the animals through the doorway.

Suddenly the silence was split as two rifles spat from the house sending bullets whining unpleasantly close to the outlaw's heads.

They grabbed for their Colts and loosed off rapid shots in the direction of the house.

'Must be the old man an' the girl,' yelled Saunders. 'Let's git out of here.'

The horses, frightened by the firing, were pulling at their reins but the two men managed to keep them under sufficient control to leap into the saddles. The animals flattened themselves into a dead run and pounded away from the ranch as Manuel and Conchita fired after them without success.

Wade O'Hara kept his horse at a fast gallop along the familiar trail through the valley but once he had ridden through the section which he knew he slowed his pace. After two hours' riding he decided he would be safe and turned his horse to the shelter of some trees beside a small stream. He secured his horse to a tree and made himself comfortable for the night. Sleep did not come easily, his mind being preoccupied with the trouble in which he found himself.

Eventually he dozed but for how long he did not know. Suddenly he was wide awake. He sat up unable to say what had woken him. He glanced around trying to pierce the darkness but all seemed calm and quiet.

Wade felt uneasy and slowly climbed to his feet. When he rose to his full height he was startled to see the glow of a camp-fire further along the bank of the stream.

Wade hesitated a few moments and then decided to investigate. He moved forward cautiously and when he could make out the silhouettes of the two men near the fire he dropped to the ground and crept forward Indian fashion. Using every available cover he approached the fire until he was certain he would be able to see the two men clearly. He peered cautiously round some bushes and was startled to see Jake Saunders and Pete Corby.

Wade's thoughts raced. What had happened back at the ranch to bring Saunders and Corby out here? Did they know he had been at the ranch? Were they on his trail or was it just coincidence they had ridden this way? He inclined his head, listening intently when he realised Corby was speaking.

'I'm not happy about this fire,' he said.

'What you frightened about?' snapped Saunders. 'The Cordoba's won't bother about us, more likely they'll git after O'Hara an' thet map. Besides they'll stay with Carlos at least until daylight.'

Wade stiffened, his hand closed round his

Colt. So they knew about him and the map ... but Carlos, what had they done to Carlos? Wade pulled his Colt from its holster. He hesitated. It would be so easy to shoot the two men without their knowing but somehow Wade could not bring himself to a cold-blooded murder. He pushed the gun back into its leather and moved carefully away from the bushes. As he turned his foot caught a stone sending it clattering across the hard ground. He froze in his tracks, hardly daring to breathe.

The two men at the fire stopped speaking. They looked up, their hands moving to their Colts.

'What was thet?' whispered Corby.

The silence was suddenly split as Saunders laughed raucously.

'Quiet,' snapped Corby, but his companion continued to laugh.

'Your face,' gasped Saunders, his words mingling with the laughter. 'You look as if you'd seen a ghost – scared stiff. Relax, it's only some animal.'

O'Hara waited until he was sure the men had settled down again before he crept steadily back to his horse. He unhitched the animal and led it through the darkness until he was satisfied it was safe enough to climb into the saddle. He rode steadily throughout the night but as dawn began to lighten the sky to the east he sought the shelter of a group of rocks some distance from the obvious trail. There he spent an uneasy day and in the evening once more headed in a southerly direction. The following morning he camped early and having seen no further sign of his former partners decided that it would now be safe to travel by day and sleep by night. He toyed with the idea of re-turning to El Rancho Sierra de Espuma but came to the conclusion that when Saunders and Corby failed to pick up his trail they would anticipate his return to the Cor-dobas. Wade cursed the luck which had suddenly shattered his dream of peace with the girl he loved and left him with map of a gold mine he did not want.

The gold mine! Wade suddenly realised that here was his chance to help the Cordobas. He felt indebted to them and now whilst he had this map why not turn it to advantage? He would return with gold and then if Saunders and Corby showed up again he would face them with his gun.

Wade now rode with more purpose, swung westwards so that he would be well away from the Cordoba lands when he headed northwards. He avoided all contact with humans but after days of wearying travel he realised that he must replenish his supplies and rest up for a while.

The trail took him into a small Mexican town of Ascension and as he rode slowly into the town square the dust-covered American on a weary horse roused the curiosity of the peons who lounged in the shade. He failed to notice one man who climbed to his feet when he saw Wade swing out of the saddle in front of the small *cantina*. O'Hara slouched into the building and slumped into a chair beside a small table. He took off his Stetson and after slapping dust from it he dropped it on to another chair. A fat man with a dirty apron tied round his middle shuffled from the counter and crossed to Wade's table where he took the newcomer's order.

Weary with travel Wade took no notice of the few other occupants of the room. When the frigoles, tortillas and eggs arrived he gave the first substantial meal he had had since riding from El Rancho Sierra de Espuma so much attention that he failed to notice the two Mexicans who entered the café and watched him as they leaned against the counter.

When he had finished his meal Wade

pushed himself from the table, threw some money on to the counter and strolled from the *cantina*. He unhitched his horse from the rail and led it towards the small wooden-fronted hotel unaware that two Mexicans left the *cantina* to watch his movements.

O'Hara fastened his horse to the rail outside the hotel and walked inside where he booked a room.

'If you like a bath, *señor*, I heat some water,' offered the thin, pale-faced proprietor.

'Thanks,' replied Wade. He smiled at the small boy standing beside his father. 'You like to earn a silver dollar?' he asked. He laughed when he saw the youngster's eyes brighten. 'My horse is out front,' went on Wade, 'you take good care of him an' the dollar is yours.'

'*Si, señor*, I take good care of him. We have our own stable round the back,' replied the boy and raced from the hotel.

The proprietor showed Wade to his room and shortly afterwards the cowboy was enjoying the luxury of a hot bath unaware that his movements had been to the satisfaction of the two observant Mexicans. They knew where their man would be when they wanted to contact him.

SIX

An hour later Wade was laying on his bed when the door of his room opened and two Mexicans with drawn guns slipped quietly inside. Startled, the cowboy automatically made a move for his Colt which was hanging in its holster on the bed head.

'No, *señor*, that wouldn't be wise.' The Mexican's voice was quiet but firm.

Wade stopped his movement and lay back on the bed observing the two men who confronted him. He saw the one who had spoken was the taller and older of the two. Wade put his age about fifty and in spite of the excess fat which now filled his body the cowboy could see that he had been a powerful man when he was younger, similar to the young man who stood by his side and whom Wade reckoned was the older man's son due to the likeness in their faces. Both men stepped forward to the bed, their guns still covering Wade unwaveringly.

'I am sorry to intrude in this way, *Señor* O'Hara but I must ask you to come with us.'

The older man's voice was pleasant enough and Wade looked at him curiously.

'How do you know my name and what do you want with me?' he asked.

Both men smiled. 'You have nothing to fear from us,' continued the older man.

'The influence of the Cordobas is widespread and I believe you possess something which rightfully belongs to *Señor* Manuel Cordoba. It is his wish that we prevent you from using it for your own good. You must come with us and you will be returned to the Cordobas.'

Wade was surprised that Manuel should go to such lengths. 'I did everything for the good of the family,' replied Wade, 'and if I return it could bring trouble back to them.'

'We know nothing of that, *señor*,' came the firm reply. 'We only obey *Señor* Manuel's orders.'

Wade could see it would be useless to try to reason with the two men. He looked hard at them. 'What if I refuse?' he asked.

The Mexican smiled and shrugged his shoulders. 'With two guns covering you what can you do and a little tap on the head would make everything certain, now, please, *señor*, don't make things difficult.'

'They won't be!' snapped a voice from the

doorway. 'Hold it,' the voice rapped again as the Mexicans started to turn. They froze where they were. 'Right, O'Hara take their guns.'

Wade, amazed at hearing an American accent leaped from the bed, relieved the two men of their guns and moved to see his rescuer. He was surprised when he saw a short, stocky man whose face, in spite of the thick growth of moustache and beard, showed every indication of a life spent in the open. It was brown and weather-beaten, almost leathery in its appearance and although it was hard to judge Wade estimated his age to be over sixty. His clothes were old and worn and to the young man he looked every inch a prospector but the thing which caught Wade's attention were the sharp, bright eyes which seemed to be able to size up a situation at a glance.

'Thanks,' grinned Wade.

There was no answering smile from the old man. 'Fergit it,' he replied seriously, his eyes never leaving the Mexicans. 'We'll hev these two tied up. Git the sheets off the bed.' Wade did as he was told and after the sheets had been removed the old man spoke to the two Mexicans. 'Gomez, Philipe, on the bed,' he ordered and when they hesitated he motioned with his gun.

Father and son climbed on to the bed and Wade set about tying them up. He had been surprised when the old man had addressed them by name but he was even more surprised when the man known as Gomez spoke.

'*Señor* Jeb,' he said, 'you shouldn't do this, you will regret it.'

The old man scowled. 'I don't like doin' this,' he muttered, 'but I can't see you treat a Yanki in this way.'

'You will not be welcome in this town again, *señor*,' answered Gomez. '*Señor* Cordoba will...'

'Shut up,' snapped the old man. 'You'll hev me changin' my mind. Hurry up,' he added glancing at Wade, 'or maybe I will.'

When Wade had Gomez and his son securely tied and gagged the old man slipped his Colt back into its holster, stepped forward and examined Wade's handiwork. He grunted with satisfaction.

'Come on,' he said, 'let's git out of here.'

Wade said nothing, thankful that he had been saved from an awkward situation. There would be time for questions later. He grabbed his gun-belt and quickly fastened it in position. Picking up the rest of his belongings he followed the old man out of the room. He led the way down some rickety stairs and Wade found himself outside the back of the hotel.

'Git your horse, son,' instructed the prospector, 'an' meet me out front; I'm all ready to ride.' His tone was much friendlier and Wade hurried to do his bidding without question.

He ran to the building which was obviously the stable and found the proprietor's son still rubbing the animal.

'Saddle up,' instructed Wade.

'But, *señor*, I've not finished yet,' protested the boy. 'I thought you were staying here.'

'I've met a friend who wants me to ride with him,' lied Wade. 'You've done a good job,' he went on eyeing the animal, 'you've earned your dollar.' He put his hand into his pocket and passed the coin to the boy whose face was split by a broad grin.

'*Gracias, señor,*' he said. 'I have him saddled in no time at all.'

A few minutes later Wade rode into the main street where he joined his rescuer. The old man turned his horse and pack horse without a word and walked the animals slowly along the street. Wade felt the urge to put his mount into a gallop and get as far as he could before the two Mexicans were discovered but he controlled his feeling and matched the pace of the older man.

Once clear of town the prospector quickened the pace and gradually increased it until they were riding at a fast gallop. Still he did not speak, nor did he seem to bother about the man beside him but Wade felt compelled to follow him. After about an hour's hard riding they left the trail and the old man led the way along an arroyo for about two miles before climbing out of it and crossing some rough scrub towards a low range of hills. They reached them about an hour later and climbing the first hill the prospector paused before reaching the top. He shaded his eyes and meticulously searched the countryside across which they had travelled.

Satisfied with what he saw he grunted and to Wade, who watched him carefully, he seemed to visibly relax. The tension which had gripped the man since he had entered Wade's room in the hotel seemed to flow out of his body. He looked at Wade and smiled and the young man saw friendliness in the lined face. He realised he was seeing the true man, a friendly, old prospector but Wade knew from the past few hours that the man could be relentless and unswerving if the situation demanded it.

'Wal, O'Hara,' he said, 'we aren't being followed, looks as if we've given them the slip.'

Before Wade could answer he turned his horse and careful not to break the sky-line he led the way round the hill. They came into a narrow, dried-up, little valley across which the prospector led the way to a cave on the opposite hillside.

Behind the narrow entrance, which appeared to be hardly more than a split in the hillside, the cave widened out and was almost cut in two by a wall of rock.

They dismounted and Wade turned to the old man. 'Thanks, for what you've done,' he said.

'Save thet until I know if I deserve it when I hear your story,' cut in the prospector. He held out his hand. 'Jeb Carter,' he added.

Wade took the hand in a firm grip. 'Wade 'But you know thet already.'

The prospector grinned 'Let's git settled in. I found this place about five years ago an' as far as I know no one else knows about it. The horses will be fine on the other side of this wall.'

The animals were soon stripped of their saddles and harness and made comfortable. The two men quickly settled themselves in and once the fire was going Jeb soon had some coffee ready.

Wade sipped his drink and then looked at the old man. 'Wal, I guess you'll want to know my story but first settle my curiosity, how did you know about me and why did you help me? You were obviously on friendly terms with those two Mexicans.'

Jeb grinned. 'About fifteen years ago I spent some time prospectin' around here,' he explained. 'I got to know the town an' was on friendly terms with the people – as a matter of fact I've seen Philipe grow up. I often come back fer a bit of peace an' quiet especially when the Indians are a bit troublesome up north. I'd been in town the past three weeks an' heard a rumour thet a certain Yanki, Wade O'Hara, was wanted by Manuel Cordoba. What for, I could not find out. I was in the *cantina* when you came in, I watched you carefully an' liked the look of you. Gomez an' Philipe came in an' when I saw the way they watched you I knew you were the man they were looking for. When you left the *cantina* they followed you out-side an' when I saw the boy take your horse I knew you were going to stay the night. I realised it would not be long before Gomez approached you an' I suppose I hed a natural instinct to help a fellow country-man. I also realised thet if I did I must be prepared to make a quick get-away so I took the risk of losing sight of Gomez to git my horses ready. I was lucky, Gomez was jest goin' into the hotel when I got back on to the street.' He paused, drank some coffee and added, 'The rest you know.'

A minute or two passed before Wade spoke. 'I'm mighty grateful for what you did,' he said, 'and I hope some day that Gomez and Philipe and the rest of your friends will not hold it against you.'

Jeb shrugged his shoulders. 'I'm jest natur-ally curious,' he said, 'an' when an American is wanted by Manuel Cordoba I sense a story.'

Wade liked the old man. He liked his frankness and sincerity and he decided to be equally open in return. The cowboy started his story and Jeb listened intently without interrupting. Wade told him every detail and when he had finished Jeb grunted and nodded as if he was weighing up all the facts.

'Thanks fer trusting me with all the de-tails, son,' said the old man. 'I appreciate thet, especially when you don't know me an' you hev the map of the fabulous Super-stition mine. I understand the reason fer your actions even though it blackened you in the eyes of the Cordobas an' I realise thet if you had returned with Gomez it would hev brought Saunders an' Corby back as well.'

'You heven't seen those two around?' asked Wade.

'Nope.' The old man shook his head then looked hard at Wade. 'What do you intend to do now?' he asked.

Wade hesitated, staring at the fire. 'I'm not sure,' he replied. 'I reckon Saunders and Corby will never let up until they git me. I've toyed with the idea of going after this gold – not for myself,' he hastened to add, 'but to help the Cordobas.'

Jeb smiled. 'I'm glad you added thet, son,' he said. 'I was 'fraid you might be after the gold fer yourself.'

'I couldn't do thet,' answered Wade, his mind full of Conchita's accusing eyes.

'Know anythin' about gold in the Superstitions?' asked Jeb.

Wade shook his head.

'How about lettin' me help you?' suggested Jeb. 'I've been a prospector all my life, an' a great part of the time I've spent in Arizona, I've even been in the Superstitions. If you don't know that part of the country you'll need some help; the land can kill you an' the Apaches are none too friendly especially if they're on the war path!'

SEVEN

Wade took readily to Jeb's suggestion realising that two probably stood a better chance than one in the country which lay ahead. He felt he could trust Jeb and knew that Jeb's knowledge would be a great asset to him.

'I can make no bargain with you,' Wade told him frankly. 'If we find gold it rightly belongs to the Cordobas and I aim to see that they get it to put them back on their feet again. No doubt *Señor* Manuel will see you get your just share.'

Jeb grinned at this. 'I'm not interested in gold for its value; as long as I find some and keep myself going with a bit I'm happy. I don't want a fortune, never hev. It's the thrill of searchin' an' findin'; the outdoor, open-air life; never tied down; with only myself to please thet I like. I'm happy to be headin' into the Superstitions with you but

I'll warn you it will be a rough tough journey an' the Superstitions themselves are no picnic at the end of it.'

'Thanks,' said Wade. 'I'm proud to hev you with me. All I'm interested in is proving to Conchita that she was wrong about me and by helping the Cordobas I hope it will put you right with the folks in Ascension.'

The two men laid up in the cave for three days, letting the hue and cry die down, and resting for the journey ahead. They pulled out of the cave in the early hours of the fourth day intending to travel in the coolness of the morning and evening and rest during the heat of the day. Jeb kept to a steady pace conserving the strength of both animals and men as they crossed the arid land towards the border.

Nearing the border Jeb asked Wade if he had ever been in Tombstone.

'No,' replied Wade with a shake of his head.

'I wish we hadn't to go there,' said Jeb seriously, 'but we'll hev to pick up fresh supplies before headin' fer the Superstitions. It's a rough, tough town, so watch yourself,' he warned. 'Mind you it's not as rough as it was in its early days when miners swarmed in from all over the world an' the Lucky Cuss,

Tough Nut an' Goodenough mines were pourin' out their wealth. The town is settlin' down after the Earp–Clanton feud a year or so back.'

'Are the mines still operating?' asked Wade.

'Some are,' answered Jeb. 'Underground water's the trouble an' miners an' prospectors are gradually pullin' out. Town'll soon be a ghost town but there lies our trouble.'

Wade looked at him curiously.

'Wal, there's still sufficient folks around fer it to be a tough spot an' with men lookin' fer fresh fields they'd slit your throat fer thet map.' The old man looked thoughtful. 'If you'd trust me with it I think I know a place where it would be safe in Tombstone.'

Wade looked doubtfully at the old man and then, when he realised the suspicion which must be in his eyes, he regretted his hesitation. He thrust his hand into a pocket and passed the map over to Jeb.

Jeb smiled but said nothing.

They moved steadily northwards and Jeb kept his eyes and ears open for signs of Indians and, although they saw none, it was some relief when Tombstone came in sight.

Wade was curious, he had heard so much about the town from Jeb, how in its heyday but a few years ago two out of every three buildings in the business area had been gambling-dens or saloons, how Jeb had been in town when Wyatt Earp and his brothers had shot it out with the Clantons at the O.K. Corral. He heard about the Bird Cage Theatre, the Crystal Palace, the Oriental Bar and the Can Can Restaurant and looked forward eagerly to seeing these places whose future was tied to the operation of the neighbouring mines.

It was early evening when they reached the town and rode slowly along Allen Street. Men thronged the boardwalks, miners in to spend their hard-earned money, those who had struck it rich to celebrate, and those who always follow the gold to make easy money out of those who worked it.

'Thought you said this town was finished,' said Wade.

'Shore,' replied Jeb. 'It soon will be but there's still plenty to keep it a rip-roarin', wild town so watch who you talk to an' what you say an' don't git liquored up.'

They made their way to Toughnut Street and pulled up outside an adobe building along the front wall of which was the name Russ House. The two men slipped from the saddles, tied their horses to the rail and went inside. They came into a large room, at one side of which was a counter whilst a number of tables and chairs were scattered around the rest of the room. Several men were sitting about the room but Wade took little notice of them. The person who caught his eye was the middle-aged lady who stood behind the counter and looked up when they entered the building. She held her well-proportioned figure erect and was well dressed in a simple way. Her fair hair was piled tidily on her head and she showed a row of white even teeth when she smiled on recognising Jeb.

'Jeb, Jeb Carter, glad to see you back again,' she called. Her soft voice carried without shouting.

The two men crossed the room and Jeb's face was wreathed in smiles as he took the lady's outstretched hand. 'It's good to see you too, Nellie,' he said. He saw her glance past him at Wade. 'Want you to meet my friend here, Wade O'Hara,' he went on. 'Wade, meet Nellie Cushman who runs Russ House.'

'Glad to meet you m'am,' said Wade removing his sombrero and taking her extended hand.

'A friend of Jeb's is a friend of mine,' she greeted pleasantly. 'Glad to know you.'

Wade saw that her eyes were deep blue and he knew that they missed nothing. He felt immediately deep respect for Nellie Cushman and he guessed that every man, no matter how rough, would feel the same in her presence. His feeling was confirmed by Jeb who went on talking.

'Nellie's never let a man go hungry in Tombstone; she's even turned this place into a hospital an' done the nursin'; she's the angel of Tombstone an' everyone has a great admiration an' respect for Nellie.'

'Shut up, Jeb,' said Nellie, her face reddening slightly at the praise. 'Are you staying the night?' she asked.

'Three nights if you can accommodate us,' said Jeb.

'Sure I can,' replied Nellie, 'and there'll be a meal on the table for you in a quarter of an hour.'

'Thanks,' said Jeb. He lowered his voice. 'But first we'd like a private word with you.'

Nellie looked at the two men curiously. 'Certainly,' she said. 'Come round here.'

Jeb and Wade moved round the counter and Nellie led the way into a small room which Wade saw was obviously used as an office.

'What's the mystery, Jeb?' asked the owner of Russ House.

'No mystery, really,' answered the old

man. 'I want you to do us a favour. Have you an envelope, please?'

Nellie took an envelope from a desk and passed it to Jeb who carefully folded the map, slipped it inside and sealed the flap. He looked hard at Nellie.

'I'll be frank with you,' he said. 'I know you can keep a secret. This is a map of the lost mine of Superstition Mountain.'

A smile flashed across Nellie's face. 'Don't tell me you've fallen for this old map tale,' she laughed. 'I thought you'd seen too many of them same as I have.'

'This is the real McCoy,' replied Jeb. 'It was obtained from Manuel Cordoba who discovered the mine.' His voice carried such conviction that Nellie no longer doubted him.

Her face became serious as she studied the two men. 'I've heard of him but how come you've got it? What do you mean – obtained?'

Wade stiffened. 'It wasn't stolen,' he put in testily.

'Hold it, son, don't git on your high horse,' Jeb said hastily. 'Nellie's only being cautious; she's on the side of law an' order an' despises men who live by their guns.'

'Sorry.' Wade mumbled his apology.

'That's all right,' answered Nellie. 'But if

I'm handling something I like to know all about it. I knew Jeb wouldn't be a thief but I don't know you yet.'

'I took it from the Cordobas,' explained Wade. 'It was to save them from trouble at the hands of two ex-partners of mine.' He went on to explain briefly what had happened.

Nellie nodded thoughtfully when Wade finished. 'That piece of paper is mighty hot stuff to have around Tombstone, I reckon there's hardly a man in town who wouldn't give his right arm to possess that map.'

'Thet's why I've come to you, Nellie,' said Jeb. 'I thought you might keep it in your safe fer us.'

'Sure,' said Nellie. She took the envelope, unlocked the safe and placed it inside.

Suddenly Wade spun on his heel and in two strides was at the door which he saw had unfortunately been left ajar when they had come into the room. He jerked it open; there was no one there. He looked out but everything appeared to be the same as when they had entered Russ House. Shutting the door he turned back into the office.

'What's wrong?' asked Jeb.

'Thought I heard someone outside,' replied Wade.

'I've told you so many stories about Tombstone it's made you jumpy,' laughed the old man.

'Guess so,' grinned Wade.

'Your map will be safe with me,' said Nellie and they left the office.

As they crossed the entrance to go to their rooms Wade glanced at the men who were sitting around and made a mental note of them. When he returned a few minutes later with Jeb he saw that three of them had been joined by a fourth who grinned when he saw Jeb.

'Wal, if it ain't old Jeb Carter back again,' he called raucously. 'Thought you'd gone into Mexico. There must be something mighty temptin' to bring you back so soon.'

'Reckon I can please myself where I go, an' when, without reportin' to you, Curt Mason,' replied Jeb coldly and walked into the dining-room where a meal was ready for them.

'Do you reckon they meant anything?' asked Wade as they sat down.

'How could they?' replied Jeb. 'They can know nothin' of the map. They're a rough, tough lot an' there's nothin' they wouldn't do to git it if they knew about it.'

The two men enjoyed their meal and

when they had finished Jeb looked hard at the young cowboy opposite to him. 'Wade,' he said seriously, 'I figure it might be a good idea if you stayed indoors tonight.'

'Why?' protested Wade. 'I was figuring on seeing the town before we headed into the wild.'

'Tomorrow,' replied Jeb. 'Look at it this way. Saunders an' Corby hev probably kept the ranch under observation to see if you returned an' when you didn't they could hev figured you'd use the map an' head fer Superstition Mountain. If they reckon thet way then it's my guess they'd also surmise you'd come to Tombstone. Let me hev a look round tonight whilst you keep out of sight.'

Wade looked thoughtful. 'You could be right,' he said. 'I'll see Tombstone tomorrow.'

As he mounted the stairs to his room Wade was aware that the four men were still sitting round a table in the hall but he reassured himself with the knowledge that only three people knew that the map was in Nellie Cushman's safe.

EIGHT

When Wade had disappeared from view Curt grinned at his three companions. 'Thet was mighty smart of you, Red,' he said, 'to figure somethin' was in the wind when Jeb Carter turned up again so soon. Careless of them to leave that door open so that you heard all thet was said.'

Red grinned. 'I reckon we're in luck,' he said.

'Do you figure the map'll be genuine?' asked a dark, hook-nosed cowboy doubtfully.

'Jeb Carter must think so to git it locked in a safe, Matt,' replied the fourth man, 'an' I know an' easy way into thet safe.'

Curt looked at the speaker severely. 'Don't come out with one of your jokes, Slim, an' say the key.'

Slim smiled. 'Thet's jest what I am sayin',' he answered. 'Once asked Nellie to look after some gold dust fer me. She'd left her key upstairs but she produced a duplicate from a drawer an' put it back there.'

'Then we're on an easy thing tonight,'

grinned Curt. 'Let's go an' hev a drink to celebrate.'

The four men pushed themselves from the table and left Russ House in high spirits.

It was late when they returned and the boarding house was quiet as they pushed open the door. An old oil lamp burned dimly in the entrance, left on for any late arrivals. The four men crept quietly to the door of the office. Curt paused, listening, but there was not a sound throughout the building. He turned the knob gently and pushed the door open.

'Fetch thet lamp, Red,' he whispered.

The man did as he was told and the four men crept into the office. Slim moved round the desk and motioned to Red to bring the lamp nearer. He pulled at the top drawer only to find it locked. He cursed softly, pulled out a knife and in a matter of moments eased the lock and had the drawer open.

'Quiet!' The urgent whisper came from Matt who had remained near the door from which he kept watch whilst holding it slightly ajar.

Footsteps echoed along the boardwalk growing louder as they approached Russ House. Red shielded the light and the four men tensed themselves, hands hanging close to their Colts. The footsteps drew nearer, faltered, then seemed to be coming right into Russ House until they began to fade. The tension went out of the waiting men. Slim felt inside the drawer and with a low gasp of triumph pulled out a key. He swung round and dropping on one knee in front of the safe soon had it opened. Red was beside him holding the lamp nearer. Slim grabbed papers and envelopes from the safe and glanced through them quickly.

'No map here!' he snarled.

'It was put in an envelope,' Red reminded him.

Curt leaned forward and snatched the bundle from Slim's hand. 'Let me look,' he snapped. He turned to the desk. 'Bring the light here.'

The two men straightened and Red moved closer to Curt who threw everything to one side except four envelopes. He tore them open quickly. His face darkened when he saw the contents of the last one was not what he wanted.

'You sure they put it in the safe?' he snarled, glaring at Red. 'You ain't holdin' out on us.'

Red stiffened. 'I saw Nellie put it there,' he hissed.

'None of them saw you?' asked Curt.

'No,' replied Red. 'Thet young hombre came to the door but I was back with Slim an' Matt; he couldn't suspect anythin'.'

Slim and Matt muttered their agreement.

'It must hev been removed afterwards,' said Curt thoughtfully. 'All we can do is to keep our eyes on Jeb Carter an' his new found pal. Let's git...'

'Quiet!' Matt hissed urgently from the door. 'Someone comin'.' The unknown person had crossed the roadway and now as he mounted the steps on to the boardwalk his boots echoed loudly. He was coming into Russ House!

Red grabbed his sombrero and held it in front of the lamp. Matt's Colt was in his hand and he tensed himself as he watched a shadowy figure grope his way across the hallway towards the stairs.

The figure stopped, turned and shuffled round the counter towards the office door. Suddenly Matt recognised the newcomer and as a hand reached for the knob Matt jerked the door open, grabbed the man by the shirt and pulled him roughly inside. Taken completely unawares the man was inside the room before he realised what was happening. Following Matt's action Curt and Slim jerked their Colts from their holsters and had the new arrival covered when Red unshaded the light.

'Reckon we're mighty pleased to see Jeb Carter,' smirked Matt.

Jeb gasped with astonishment his eyes moving from the four men to the open safe.

'What goes on?' he asked sharply. 'Nellie never did you any harm.'

'Keep your voice down,' hissed Curt. 'We ain't robbin' Nellie. Her money's still in the safe, you can see fer yourself. We are interested in a map but it isn't here; maybe you were comin' fer it.'

Jeb's mind had been racing. 'Map?' he said. 'I don't know about a map, I thought it was funny when there was no light in the hall, Nellie generally leaves one. Then I saw a faint glimmer from the office an' thought she might be in here.'

'Wal, now you're here, I reckon you can tell us where to find what we're lookin' fer,' snapped Curt.

'I'm not interested in Nellie's business,' flashed back Jeb.

'It's not her business we're interested in,' replied Curt harshly. 'It's yours! Where's thet map?'

'Map?' Jeb feigned bewilderment.

'Come off it old-timer,' snapped Red. 'You know what we're talkin' about. You gave Nellie a map of the location of the lost mine of Superstition Mountain to put in her safe. I heard and saw you.'

'You must be mistaken,' returned Jeb. 'I've never had a map...'

'Wrap it up,' cut in Red angrily. 'I heard you talk about it so don't waste time denying it.'

Jeb's brain pounded. So Wade had not been mistaken when he thought he had heard someone outside the door. Red was right; it was no use denying it. But where was the map? The last time he had seen it was when Nellie had put it in the safe. Maybe Wade had collected it; but why?

Jeb looked round the four men, their faces were grim in the dim light and Jeb knew he was in a tough spot. 'Wal, as Red seems to know about it, it's no use denyin' thet there is a map,' he said quietly.

'Then what's happened to it,' snapped Red.

'Thet's what I'd like to know,' answered Jeb. 'Last time I saw it it was in thet safe.'

'I figure it wasn't,' rapped Curt. He stepped forward menacingly and relieved Jeb of his gun.

The four men slipped their guns back into

the holsters and Matt and Slim stepped forward.

'You goin' to talk?' asked Curt.'

'I've told you all I know,' answered Jeb. 'Thet map means a lot to some folk an' I'd like to know where it is.'

'So would we,' said Curt coldly, 'an' we figure on findin' out.'

Matt moved behind Jeb and pinioned his arms to his side as Slim brought the back of his hand viciously across the old man's face. The ring on Slim's finger bit into Jeb's face and blood began to run down his cheek. Jeb's head pounded as Slim brought the palm of his hand back across Jeb's other cheek. Before he realised what was happening Slim's left fist dug deep into his side sending a searing pain ripping through his middle. He gasped as the air was driven from his body and he could find no relief by doubling up as Matt held him rigid in a strong grip. Slim's right fist swung hard into the old man's stomach and Jeb felt a sickness rise inside him with the rush of pain. His head spun but suddenly he felt some relief and he realised he was no longer held in the vice-like grip. As Matt dumped him on to a chair he doubled up and would have fallen had not Matt seized the back of his shirt and held him. Curt stepped forward and pushed Jeb's head back roughly. He glanced down at the old man who was only vaguely aware of the face above him.

'Tell us, Carter, or there'll be worse than thet,' snarled Curt.

Jeb shook his head. 'I don't know,' he panted. 'I'm tellin'...'

Curt let Jeb's head go and as it slumped forward Curt's fist came up jerking it backwards and opening a long cut over Jeb's right eye. The room swam in front of him. He felt the grip relax and he could do nothing to prevent himself falling on to the floor. He jerked with pain as a boot lashed into his thigh. He tensed himself for the next blow but it never came. He heard a voice which seemed to be far away but he recognised it as Red's.

'Supposin' the old-timer is tellin' the truth,' he said, 'an' he doesn't know what's happened to the map.'

'Then who's got it,' snapped Slim. 'I reckon Carter's holdin' out on us.'

'Nellie Cushman knew it was in the safe,' pointed out Matt.

'Nellie wouldn't steal it,' replied Curt, 'she's too honest fer that.' He looked thoughtful. 'But there's thet young hombre Jeb was with,' he added. 'He could hev got it. Reckon Slim an' Matt ought to bring him down here.'

'I'm already here!' The voice was cold and menacing.

The four men spun round to face the door, their hands automatically moving towards their Colts but they froze before they touched the butts when they saw themselves staring into the cold muzzle of a Colt held in the steady hand of Wade O'Hara!

'Take this easy and no one will get hurt,' said Wade slowly, his eyes narrowing as he watched the four men closely. 'Unbuckle your gun-belts an' let them drop.'

Red, Slim and Matt glanced at Curt but his face was expressionless. It was obvious that he was not prepared to make a play for it against a man who already held the upper hand. They moved their hands slowly to their buckles and in a matter of seconds four gun-belts clattered on the floor.

Jeb Carter was struggling to get up but pain racked his body and he groaned with the effort.

'Help him,' snapped Wade to Curt.

After Curt had helped the old man on to a chair Jeb felt a little easier. 'Thanks, Wade,' he gasped.

'Will you be all right if I take these hombres

to the sheriff?' asked Wade.

'Sure, son,' answered Jeb.

'Pick up the lamp,' ordered Wade, 'an' keep close together as we move out of here an' don't try anythin' or someone will feel a bullet.' He motioned towards the door and the four men shuffled forward.

Wade was pleased to see a light still burning in the sheriff's office.

'Want you to arrest these men for attempted robbery,' said Wade and went on to explain briefly what he knew.

'I reckon we'll see they cool off in jail fer awhile,' said the sheriff when Wade finished his story. He motioned towards the cells and the four men, swearing vengeance on Wade, shuffled behind the bars.

Wade picked up the lamp which Red had put down, thanked the sheriff and hurried back to Russ House where he found Jeb still sitting in the chair but recovering his breath although his body still ached with its beating.

'I'll get Nellie,' said Wade and hurried upstairs to return a few moments later.

Nellie gasped when she saw the open safe and the bruised and blood-spattered Jeb. The old man started to speak but she halted him. 'Save it,' she said. 'I'll fix you up first.'

She hurried away but soon returned with some hot water and clean cloths and gently and efficiently bathed Jeb's wounds. When she was satisfied that everything was to her liking she sought an explanation.

'I spent an uneasy night,' said Wade, 'and finally I got up to go to see Jeb. I found he wasn't in his room and I was worried in case anything had happened to him. I was going to look for him but when I came downstairs I saw a light in the office. I investigated, found the safe open, Jeb beaten up and Curt Mason and three sidekicks about to come for me.'

Jeb told his story and when he had finished he looked anxiously at Nellie. 'They couldn't find the map; what's happened to it?'

Nellie smiled. 'I was uneasy when Wade thought he heard someone at the door when we were talking about the map,' she explained, 'so I decided not to leave it in the safe, I took it upstairs to my room and that's where it is now.'

Relief spread across Jeb's face. 'Thank goodness you did or those four coyotes would hev hed it now. I reckon we'll git our supplies together in the mornin' an' pull out of here.'

'Oh no you don't,' put in Nellie emphatically. 'You won't be fit to travel.' Jeb started to protest but Nellie would not listen to him. 'Wade, keep him quiet until I bring Doc Jones; he'll tell you when you can travel.'

The doctor examined Jeb carefully and reported that although he was badly bruised no serious injury had been sustained but he insisted that Jeb spend two days in bed.

'Wal, Wade,' said Jeb when he was in bed, 'I won't be able to show you the town tomorrow. Nobody answering your description of Saunders an' Corby hev been seen but watch your step.'

NINE

Two cowboys swung slowly from their saddles in front of the Oriental Saloon on the corner of Allen Street and Fifth Street in Tombstone. They strolled on to the sidewalk and paused as the thunder of hoofs heralded the approach of a stagecoach. The driver pulled hard on the reins and pushed on the brake handle with his foot to bring the swaying coach to a halt further along the street. Already people were hurrying to meet it and the two men leaned on the rail watching them closely.

'We'll drift along to the Can Can Restaurant later an' see if they still run fresh lobsters up by the fast stage from Cuayman,' drawled Jake Saunders. 'C'm on, let's shake...'

His words were cut short by Pete Corby as he grabbed his arm. 'There he is!' hissed Pete.

Jake stiffened and followed Pete's gaze to see Wade O'Hara hurrying along the sidewalk on the opposite side of the street.

'You were right,' he said.

'Of course,' replied Jake, a note of triumph in his voice. 'I figured he wouldn't return to the ranch with the map to a fortune in his pocket an' he was bound to call here fer supplies. Guess we timed it right.'

Pete straightened, his hand closing round the butt of the Colt. 'Let's git him, then,' he hissed, his eyes disclosing his hate for the man on the opposite side of the street.

Jake's hand closed round Corby's. 'Don't be a fool,' he snapped. 'Tombstone may be a rough town but it's not like it used to be when you could git away with a thing like that.'

'We owe that coyote fer our years in prison,' snarled Corby.

'I aren't fergittin' thet,' answered Saunders, 'but we want thet map an' when we can git it without drawin' attention to ourselves we'll kill two birds with one stone, besides we want to make sure he's got it on him.'

Corby began to see sense in his partner's words and they strolled casually along Allen Street keeping Wade in sight. He called at two stores before turning into Fourth Street. The two men followed him and when they saw him turn into Toughnut Street they ran to the corner.

'Guess he's headin' fer Nellie Cushman's place,' said Saunders. He quickened the pace to close the distance between them and when O'Hara turned into Russ House Saunders and Corby were close on his heels.

Saunders pushed the door slightly open and when he saw Wade hurrying up the stairs he stepped inside.

'Sit down there an' read the *Epitaph*,' he whispered to Corby. 'I'll be back in a minute.'

Jake hurried up the stairs and was just in time to see Wade's broad back disappearing into a room. He strolled along the corridor, paused outside the door and hearing voices he moved further along the passage. A few moments later he heard a door open and, glancing over his shoulder, saw Wade come out and enter the adjoining room. Jake spun round and walked quickly to the door through which he had seen Wade O'Hara disappear. He paused, listening intently, and hearing only the movements of Wade he was satisfied he had found the room he was looking for.

Jake hurried down the stairs and sat down beside Pete Corby.

'Found his room,' he whispered. 'We'll sit tight here an' when he comes out we'll search his room fer the map, if it isn't there then we know he's got it on him.'

'Why not go an' git it now?' asked Corby.

'An' cause an uproar,' snapped Saunders. 'If thet happened then we couldn't keep the fact of the map a secret. We'll sit here all day an' night if needs be. Now git your head in thet paper an' don't let him see you when he comes out.'

Saunders picked up another copy of the *Epitaph* and the two men appeared to interest themselves in the newspapers but kept a wary eye on the stairs.

An hour passed before the sound of footsteps caused Saunders to glance over the top of his paper. He nudged Corby and they saw O'Hara cross the hall and go out into the street. They waited a few moments, put down their papers and strolled casually to the staircase. Once they reached the corridor Saunders hurried forward and as a precautionary measure tapped lightly on the door. Receiving no reply he opened the door and the two men stepped inside.

'Keep it quiet,' whispered Jake. 'Wade knows someone in the next room.'

The two men swiftly and systematically searched the room.

'There's nothin' here,' snarled Corby angrily when he realised their search was useless. 'I told you we should hev taken him in here.'

'Use your head,' snapped back Saunders. 'Now we know he must hev the map on him. We'll pick him up an' deal with him in an alley.'

They left the room, hurried out of Russ House, turned the corner into Fifth Street and walked down to Allen Street. Luck was with them; as they strolled along the sidewalk, their eyes searching everywhere for O'Hara, they saw him emerge from the Can Can Restaurant and walk slowly along to the Crystal Palace Saloon. The two men crossed the dusty street, pushed through the door and saw Wade cross to the long mahogany bar. Saunders and Corby moved to the gambling tables which girded the walls and which were crowded with miners and cowboys. They mingled with the throng round the roulette table and took up a position from which they could watch Wade.

The young cowboy took his time enjoying several glasses of beer and when he decided to leave the Crystal Palace it was dark. Saunders and Corby followed him across Allen Street.

'He's headin' fer the Bird Cage,' Saunders informed his partner but for some reason Wade changed his mind when he reached the wooden-fronted building.

He paused then walked on and turned into Sixth Street. The street was quiet and Saunders and Corby quickly closed the distance between themselves and O'Hara. The two men drew their guns and when Wade reached an alley half way along the street they closed alongside him.

Before he knew what was happening he was bundled into the alley and a Colt cracked down on his head. The young man pitched forward into the dust and lay still.

Corby slipped his Colt back into its leather, and swiftly searched the silent form. Suddenly he straightened. 'There's no map here,' he snarled angrily as he jerked his gun from its holster.

'Hold it!' snapped Saunders.

'If we can't git the map then I'll hev revenge fer what he did to us,' hissed Corby.

'Don't be a fool,' threw back Saunders. 'If you kill him we'll never git the map; it must be somewhere. Leave him here; he won't feel like leavin' town tonight; we'll put the tabs on him again tomorrow.' He grabbed Corby by the arm and turned him away. Corby resisted momentarily then, realising Saunders was right, he slipped his Colt back into its holster and the two men hurried into the darkness.

Half an hour later Wade's eyes flickered open. His head throbbed as if a thousand hammers were beating inside. He lay still trying to realise what had happened and as his senses slowly cleared he rolled over pushed himself slowly to his feet. He staggered and sought support against the wooden building on his right. Putting his hand to his head he felt it gingerly; a huge lump had risen and he was aware of the sticky feel of blood. Moving forward his foot kicked his Stetson and when he bent down to pick it up his head spun. He sought the aid of the wall again, waited a few minutes and when his head cleared a little he moved out of the alley to Sixth Street. Summoning his strength he walked to Toughnut Street and a few moments later staggered into Russ House.

There was no one in the lobby but Nellie Cushman who glanced towards the door as it opened. Her eyes widened with surprised horror when she saw Wade's blood-stained, dust-covered face. Moving swiftly round the corner she helped him to her office where she quickly bathed the wound.

'You'll be all right,' she informed him, 'except for a sore head in the morning.'

'Thanks,' said Wade.

'What happened?' asked Nellie.

'I was bundled into an alley,' explained Wade. 'Next thing I knew was I was waking with a head that didn't feel like mine.'

Nellie looked puzzled. 'Any idea who it was?' she asked.

The cowboy shook his head. 'It happened so quickly I didn't see their faces.'

'Did they take anythin' from you?' queried Nellie.

'Never thought to look,' replied Wade but he quickly confirmed that nothing was missing.

'Then it can't have been robbery,' said Nellie thoughtfully. 'I wonder if Curt Mason got word to someone.'

'Possible,' said Wade. 'I'd better let Jeb know about this,' he added and thanked Nellie again.

Before going to see Jeb he went into his own room and when he had lit the lamp he gasped in amazement at what it revealed. The room was upside down and his things were scattered everywhere. Wade spun on his heels and burst into Jeb's room.

'Have you heard anyone in my room?' he asked.

'Just after you'd gone out,' answered Jeb, 'Thought you'd come back.'

'It wasn't me,' said Wade grimly. 'The room has been torn apart.'

'What!' It was Jeb's turn to be surprised. 'An' what happened to you?' he went on, indicating Wade's head.

The young cowboy quickly related what had happened. 'I reckon it means one of two things,' he concluded. 'Curt Mason got word out to someone, or Saunders and Corby are in town, spotted me, turned my room over in a search for the map, and when it wasn't there, attacked me. I'm goin' out to hev a look round.'

'Fergit it,' urged Jeb. 'You could run into trouble. We'll git out of here.'

'You're in no fit state to travel yet,' pointed out Wade. 'And I don't like working in the dark; I like to know who I'm dealing with. I won't come to any harm as long as I haven't got the map. If it was Saunders and Corby and I'd the map on me I wouldn't be standing here now.'

Jeb tried to prevail upon him to stay but Wade would not hear of it. When he left Russ House he walked down Fifth Street and on to Allen Street. He figured he must have been followed when he left the Crystal Palace and he reckoned there was a possibility that his attackers may have returned there to slake their disappointment with drink.

Wade pushed open the door and paused just inside the doorway to survey the huge room with oil paintings and mirrors adorning the walls. The room was crowded; a brisk trade at the bar kept the three bartenders busy and the gambling tables were still in full use. Wade strolled across to the bar and, leaning forward with his foot on the brass rail, called for a beer. He took his time enjoying the drink keeping his eye on the room through the mirror on the wall behind the bar.

Half an hour passed when suddenly he

tensed himself when he saw two men pushing their way towards the counter. They moved up on either side of him.

'Hello, Wade,' greeted Jake Saunders heartily.

'Howdy, Wade.' Pete Corby seemed equally pleased to see him.

O'Hara eyed them suspiciously. 'You seem mighty pleased to see me,' he said.

'Of course we are,' grinned Jake. 'We're willin' to let by-gones be by-gones an' pick up where we left off before we went to jail.'

Wade's eyes narrowed. 'This is a sudden change of feeling,' he said, 'considering that not long ago you were willing to kill me.'

'Wal, you know how it is,' said Corby. 'Time makes one forget.'

'You've forgotten quickly,' snapped Wade. 'You were still hunting me when you were at the Cordoba ranch. You got on my trail mighty quick the night I left.' The two men glanced at each other. 'Yes, I saw you that night,' Wade went on, 'but I kept movin' when I saw your camp fire.' He paused, his eyes glinting as he stared hard at his two former partners. 'So why all this friendliness?' he hissed. 'What are you after?'

Saunders grinned. 'All right, Wade,' he said. 'You can hev it straight.' He lowered his voice. 'We know you've got the map to the lost mine of Superstition Mountain an' we figure three would stand a better chance of gettin' thet gold than one.'

'I've already got a partner,' replied Wade quietly.

'So he's got the map!' Corby gasped half to himself. Wade turned sharply looking hard at Corby.

'What do you mean?' he said. 'Why shouldn't I have the map?'

'Wal I don't...' spluttered Corby regretting his slip of the tongue as Wade grasped him tightly by the shirt front.

'So you've looked for it already tonight,' hissed Wade. 'First my room and then me. I've a good mind to run you both in to the sheriff.' He pushed Corby away from him roughly with a grunt of disgust.

'Fergit thet, Wade,' said Jake hastily, trying to smooth things over. 'It was only natural we should try to split two ways instead of three. Come on, count your old pals in, we're willin' to split four ways.'

'Nothing doing,' answered Wade. 'I'm not in this for my own ends.'

'Don't kid us,' rapped Corby scornfully.

'Whatever gold I find is for the Cordobas,' replied Wade. 'I intend to repay them for what they did for me. They saved me from the desert and nursed me back to health. I was there some time before you two showed up and spoiled everything for me. When I overheard you plan to steal the map there was no time to explain to the Cordobas. I just had to beat you to it. Now they think I'm a thief.'

Corby laughed. 'Wal it serves you right. I'll bet you had a right time with thet dainty Conchita. How does she...'

His words were cut short as Wade's fist crashed into his face sending him sprawling on the floor. Saunders crouched and went for his gun but Wade was too fast and like a flash of lightning a Colt appeared in his hand.

'Keep right away from thet,' he snapped. 'You too, Corby!'

A quietness had descended on the saloon in the immediate vicinity of the three men.

Wade's eyes blazed. 'I don't want to gun you two,' he said. His voice was cold, his face black with anger. 'So keep out of my way; next time it won't be so easy to let you two off.' He turned and strode towards the door pushing his Colt back into its leather.

Corby started to reach for his gun but Saunders stopped him. 'Fool,' he snapped. 'Not here. Besides,' he whispered as he dragged his partner to his feet, 'we want thet gold. We can fix him later!'

'We can't keep on his tail all the time,' said Corby. 'How are we goin' to know when he leaves town?'

'Soon fix thet,' replied Jake. 'C'm on.'

The two men strode from the Crystal Palace and walked down Allen Street to the Mexican quarter between First and Second Street. They had no difficulty in finding two Mexican boys to whom Jake described Wade O'Hara.

'This man is staying at Russ House,' concluded Jake. 'There's a dollar each if you let us know immediately he leaves town.'

The two boys looked at each other, their eyes bright at the mention of money.

'*Si, señor,* we tell you,' they replied.

'We'll be at the Cosmopolitan, room ten,' said Jake. 'Take it in turns to sleep an' don't slip up.'

The two boys scurried away to take up their positions near the entrance to Russ House.

When Wade left the Crystal Palace he hurried to Russ House and quickly informed Jeb of his encounter with his ex-partners.

'We must get out of here,' said Jeb. 'Too many people know about this map an' if any of them talk…! We must leave tonight.'

'You aren't fit to travel,' pointed out Wade. 'Besides we haven't got our supplies yet.' Jeb looked annoyed. 'I'll get them in the morning,' went on Wade, 'and get everything ready; we'll leave tomorrow night after dark and that will give you another day's rest.'

As much as Jeb argued he could not alter Wade's mind and at last the old man had to agree that Wade's was probably the best course.

The following morning after Jeb had given him a list of things they required Wade left Russ House and visited several stores unaware that his movements were being followed closely by two Mexican boys. During the afternoon he got the horses ready in the livery stable and as he was returning to Russ House he was suddenly aware of two Mexicans who had swung down from their horses and now barred his path. Wade glanced sharply at them.

'Gomez! Philipe!' he gasped.

They both smiled. '*Señor* O'Hara,' said Gomez pleasantly, 'how pleased and relieved we are to see you.'

Wade looked hard at the two men. 'If you've come to force me back, don't try it,' he warned menacingly.

'We are not here to do that,' said Gomez

quietly but firmly. 'We reported to *Señor* Cordoba after you escaped us in Ascension. He knows of Jeb Carter and thought you would head for Superstition Mountain through Tombstone; he sent us to try to persuade you to return with the map.'

Philipe noticed Wade rest his hand on the butt of his Colt. He smiled. 'There will be no violence; *Señor* Cordoba warned us not to run foul of the law north of the border. We have to try to make you see reason.'

'It is no good,' replied Wade a slight note of sadness in his voice. 'I cannot return yet, it would only bring trouble to the Cordobas and I do not want that.'

'Have you not brought trouble already, by taking the map,' said Gomez. 'Please, *señor,* come back; it will be better for everyone. *Señor* Cordoba does not wish any harm to befall you.'

'I'm sorry,' answered Wade. 'I cannot come back now, but I will one day.'

'Will you, *señor?*' Gomez sounded very doubtful.

'I will,' replied Wade emphatically. 'Tell the Cordobas that Saunders and Corby are in Tombstone, if I come back now they will only find out and follow me and then great harm will be done. Besides the Cordobas think me a thief; especially Conchita, I could read it in her eyes when I left, if I returned now they would still think the same. I must clear myself in their eyes by returning of my own accord at the right time.'

'Then you still mean to go to Superstition Mountain?' queried Philipe.

Wade nodded.

'If you do we will never see you again,' said Gomez. 'That mountain is evil and, if you find the gold, greed will come upon you. May I make one last appeal and offer you one last warning sent by *Señor* Cordoba. He asks you to remember what he told you about Superstition Mountain. He is certain there is no good there and that the Mountain will take its revenge upon you. *Señor,* I beg of you in the name of *Señor* Cordoba, do not go to Superstition Mountain.' Gomez's face was grim as he emphasised his words.

'I am sorry, Gomez,' started Wade, 'if I don't go...'

His words were interrupted by the thunder of hoofs pounding into town along Allen Street. The rider was covered in dust; his face was grim; his clothes were tattered and his right thigh was bare, revealing an ugly wound caked with dust and congealed blood. There was a look of alarm and fear in his eyes. People stared as he thundered past and then ran towards him as he hauled hard on the reins to bring his sweating mount to a sliding halt in front of the sheriff's office.

'The Apaches are rising in the north,' he yelled. 'There's blood and flame across the country. Everywhere there's...' The words choked in his throat. His body shook as he coughed and spat blood. Willing hands reached for him, helped him out of the saddle and laid him gently on the sidewalk as people crowded round and someone ran for the doctor.

Gomez turned to Wade. His face was serious. '*Señor*,' he said softly. 'The mountain has already started; those Indians are between you and Superstition Mountain!'

TEN

Gomez and Philipe turned from Wade, climbed into their saddles and rode slowly along Allen Street out of Tombstone. Wade watched them go with mixed feelings and then hurried to Russ House where he mounted the stairs quickly and went straight to Jeb

Carter's room.

Jeb frowned when Wade told him of the Indian trouble. 'This puts a new light on things,' he said seriously. 'It may be a big uprising or localised outbreaks but whichever it is it spells danger to us.'

'You've been in those parts before,' said Wade. 'Don't you know these Indians?'

'I know some of the Apache tribes,' replied Jeb, 'but thet's no guarantee of safety.' Wade looked thoughtful as Jeb paused. 'It's up to you, Wade; if you still want to go I'm with you. I'll not back out because of Indian trouble.'

'Thanks, Jeb,' replied Wade, his eyes reflecting his appreciation of Jeb's support. 'I do still want to go. Time may be running out for the Cordobas, I know things were bad with them but if they are worse than I realise, and I suspect Manuel was hiding something, then only the gold of Superstition Mountain can save them.'

Jeb smiled. 'All right, son, we'll leave tonight. Have you got everything ready?'

'Yes. I've left the horses ready at the stable,' answered Wade.

'Seen any more of Saunders and Corby?' asked the old prospector.

Wade shook his head. 'No,' he replied.

106

'And that puzzles me.'

'The fact that you out-drew them may hev scared them off,' suggested Jeb.

Wade smiled. 'They don't scare as easily as that. They're up to something or I don't know them.'

'This Indian trouble may frighten them,' said Jeb. 'It could easily give us some protection.'

'Possibly,' agreed Wade.

The two men waited in Jeb's room, until it was dark and then sought out Nellie Cushman in her office where Wade quickly explained the situation. Although Nellie tried to persuade them not to go the two men would not be put off. Nellie returned the map to them, wished them well and after saying goodbye Wade and Jeb left Russ House, hurried to the livery stables and left Tombstone unaware that their movements had aroused the curiosity of two Mexican boys.

As soon as they realised which way the riders were going the two boys ran as fast as they could to the Cosmopolitan. They burst through the door and before the startled clerk could stop them they mounted the stairs two at a time. Their hammering on the door of room ten brought Jake Saunders hurrying across the room.

'They've gone, *señor!*' panted one boy when the door opened.

'Good work,' said Saunders turning back into the room. The two boys shuffled forward. 'Which way?' he asked.

A startled clerk appeared in the doorway. 'Come on, you boys, out of here,' he ordered in a squeaky voice. 'I'm sorry about this...' he started to apologise to Jake.

'Get out!' snapped Jake. 'I told these boys to come here.'

'Oh!' The man's eyes widened with surprise. 'I'm sorry, I ... I was... Oh!'

As Jake pulled a Colt from its holster and snapped back the hammer the clerk turned and fled down the corridor. Jake and Pete laughed raucously and the boys stared in amazement.

'Wal,' said Pete impatiently, 'which way did they go?'

'West out of Allen Street and then swung north,' answered one boy.

'You sure?' asked Pete seriously. He looked at Jake. 'I thought this Indian trouble would hold them in town.'

'We're sure, *señor,*' came the definite reply.

The two men said no more but quickly gathered up their belongings and strode towards the door.

'Our payment, please, *señor.*' The boys held out their hands.

Jake and Pete looked down on the two Mexicans, then at each other and started to laugh. They stepped forward through the doorway.

'But, *señor,* you agreed,' protested the older boy.

Jake and Pete pushed the Mexicans roughly out of the way and strode down the corridor. The boys ran after them shouting angrily that they wanted payment. Suddenly Pete spun round and jerked his Colt from its holster. The boys shrank back. Pete turned and followed Jake down the stairs laughing loudly. The boys waited until the two men were out of the building before they went into the street. They wandered aimlessly, chattering loudly and heaping curses on Saunders and Corby.

'Hello there, what's the matter with you two?' The boys were startled by the voice and looking up saw someone peering between the upright bars of a window at the back of the jail.

'Why are you angry?' the man asked again.

'Two no good Yankis offer to pay us to watch other two Yankis and tell them when they rode out of town. We do jist that but get no pay,' explained one boy angrily.

'What were these two men like?' asked the prisoner. 'Maybe I will catch up with them one day and get the dollars for you,' he added with a grin.

The boy described Saunders and Corby and when pressed also described Wade and Jeb.

The prisoner smiled and threw down two dollars. 'Maybe thet will help,' he said.

The boys grabbed at the money and shouting their thanks raced down the street.

Curt Mason turned from the cell window and grinned at his fellow prisoners. 'Hear thet?' he said. 'Carter an' his partner have ridden out. There's only one place they're headin' fer – Superstition Mountain and gold!'

'Fat lot of good thet is to us in here,' snarled Slim.

'There's no need fer us to take it lying down,' answered Curt. 'Trouble with you is you don't look ahead; I've been figurin' on how to get out of here from the moment thet door slammed behind us.' He lowered his voice and when Slim, Red and Matt gathered round him he outlined his plan.

Ten minutes later Red fell to the ground moaning.

'Deputy! Deputy! Red's ill!' yelled Curt. 'Bring your keys, quick.'

The deputy sheriff automatically grabbed his keys at the urgent call and ran to the cell. Suddenly he pulled up, suspicion crossing his mind. He could see through the bars, which formed the walls of the cell, that Red was lying on the floor with Matt and Slim standing over him.

'Thet man was all right a few minutes ago,' said the deputy. 'You aren't pulling a fast one?'

Red rolled and moaned, holding his side.

'Can't you see the man's seriously ill,' snapped Curt. 'Get the doctor.'

The deputy eyed Curt suspiciously and stepped forward to have a closer look. Curt seized his chance. Reaching between the bars he grabbed the deputy's shirt and pulled him forward forcing him hard against the iron bars. In a flash Slim grabbed the keys from the man's hand and Matt seized his gun. Slim unlocked the cell door and Matt stepped outside menacing the deputy with his own gun. Curt grinned and let go of the shirt as Red jumped to his feet with a raucous laugh.

'Git inside,' ordered Matt.

The deputy hesitated but the pressure of

cold steel in his back warned him not to attempt anything foolish. He stepped into the cell and Matt whipped the gun barrel across the deputy's head. He sank to the floor without a sound. Slim locked the door, threw the keys on to the sheriff's desk and after retrieving their own guns the four men stepped out into the night.

They walked quickly along the street to the livery stable where the stable boy was unceremoniously dealt with and left unconscious in one of the stalls. Four horses were saddled quickly and Curt led the way from the stable to the back of a store which was in darkness. With little noise they broke into the building, took the supplies they needed and made their way swiftly to the west end of town where they swung north galloping into the night.

ELEVEN

It was late the following afternoon when Wade and Jeb first came across evidence of the Indian trouble; the blackened remains of what had once been a neat house in a pleasant part of the San Pedro valley.

The two men searched for a while but could find no trace of the occupants.

'Let's hope they left before the Apaches hit them,' said Jeb, 'otherwise they'll be goin' through hell now.'

Wade shuddered at the thought of being prisoner in the hands of the war-like Apaches. They moved on with more care and that night chose a secluded spot from which their low camp fire could not be seen. The next day their progress was slower and, although Jeb said little, Wade sensed from his actions that Indians had been in the vicinity recently. It was about noon when they topped a slight rise in the valley that they saw black smoke billowing skywards some distance ahead. Wade was about to send his horse forward into a gallop when Jeb restrained him.

'Too late,' he said grimly, 'an' too far away. The Indians will have done their dirty work already; we'd only ride into any young bucks thet were hangin' behind.'

Wade saw the sense of Jeb's words and the two men waited until the smoke began to subside.

'Guess we can move, now,' said Jeb.

They rode forward slowly keeping a sharp

look out for signs of Indians. It was an hour later when the house came in sight. The gaunt limbs still smouldered, silent crosses to the three bodies which sprawled near the front of the house.

'It's been a grim fight,' observed Jeb as they swung from the saddles. He noticed Wade glancing around. 'Don't worry about the devils,' he said. 'If they had been around they would hev taken us before this.' He turned to the pack-horse and unstrapped two spades passing one to Wade. 'C'm on let's git this job over,' he added grimly.

They walked across to the corral fence and dug three graves close to it. Wade was sickened by the sight as they carried the three bodies to the graves and although he had seen it all before Jeb never ceased to be horrified by the Indians' work at such times.

'I guess they were husband and wife and son, reckon he'd be about eighteen,' Jeb spoke to break the tension as they shovelled the earth back.

'Thank goodness there was no one else,' said Wade.

'There might hev been,' replied Jeb. 'If there were any daughters the Indians may hev carried them off. They'll be treated as slaves and then may be absorbed into the tribe, become squaws an' hev families.'

Wade stared at Jeb. 'I've heard of these things but didn't realise they were true.'

Jeb smiled. 'Sure they are,' he said, 'an' I've heard tell of girls carried off when they were young who became so much Indian thet they didn't want to return to the white man's life when the chance arose.' He laughed at the look of amazement on Wade's face. 'Don't fergit this son,' he went on seriously. 'Indians aren't all savage, they're a fine race, maybe they take some understanding but then I guess we do too. Wouldn't we fight if our land an' homes were threatened? An' remember this, all races hev a cruel streak in them an' the Indian learned a lot of bad habits from the white man. Indians hev been sold into slavery before today.' He paused to wipe the sweat from his wrinkled forehead. 'Mind you, I'm not defendin' them for what they've done,' Jeb added, 'but don't fergit if we run across them the Indian has a point of view.'

Jeb had given Wade something to think about and they finished their unpleasant task in silence. The young cowboy erected three crude crosses and then the two men swung into the saddles and turned their backs on the site of destruction.

They rode for about two miles before Jeb

called a halt. 'I don't like it,' he muttered, 'too many Indian signs in the valley; I reckon we'd better pull out and take our chance over the scrub and desert lying to the west of those mountains.'

They turned out of the valley and climbed steadily over a series of ridges running north and south until they reached a huge plateau of scrub and desert which stretched as far as the eye could see. The sun was setting and Wade was amazed at the colourful beauty of a landscape which he thought would be nothing but desolation.

'It has a beauty all its own,' remarked Jeb, 'but don't be deceived, it can be a killer if you are caught out there without water.'

The two men found a suitable place to camp sheltered by huge rocks and boulders.

'Reckon we ought to keep watch tonight?' asked Wade.

'I've seen no Indian signs since we started to climb away from the San Pedro,' replied Jeb. 'I think we'd be better with a good night's sleep. The going will be harder from now on, besides I reckon a guard wouldn't be much good, if there were Indians about they could take us without much bother.'

Daylight was beginning to flood the Arizona landscape when Jeb stirred in his blankets. He rubbed his face and stretched himself but as he relaxed again he received a spine-chilling shock. Shadowy figures mingled with the rocks. Jeb was wide awake in a flash but he did not attempt to get up. Instead he glanced quickly around him and saw that they were surrounded. One figure stepped forward from the shadows and then stood still. Apache! The dreaded word flashed through Jeb's mind. He looked sharply at Wade who was just beginning to stir. If the young cowboy did anything foolish when he saw the Indian they would be dead inside a second.

'Take it easy, Wade,' whispered Jeb urgently. 'We hev visitors. An' keep your hand away from your gun,' he added emphatically.

Sleep was driven from Wade's brain by the tone of Jeb's voice. He was startled by what he saw but he made no movement.

The Indian moved forward. 'You did right to warn your friend,' he said, his voice empty of feeling. 'You now give us the pleasure of watching a slow death.'

The coldness of his voice, which filled the meaning of his last two words with horror, made Wade shudder. The Indian signalled to the rest of his band and they moved in closer to the white men, two of them removing their weapons. The leader then motioned to Jeb and Wade to get up and when they had done so Wade glanced round the Indians. There were twelve of them each armed with a rifle which they kept pointing at their captives. Their faces were grim and impassive betraying none of their feelings. Wade switched his eyes to the man who was obviously their leader. Although he was no taller than the other Apaches there was something about his personality which made the others respect and look up to him. His dark eyes were sunk in a sharp cruel face framed by the straight black hair which hung down to his shoulders and which was held by a band of cloth tied around his head. A belt was fastened round his shirt-like garment underneath which there hung to his knees a cloth which was split at the sides revealing powerful legs. His feet were covered by calf length, well-worn moccasins.

'It is as well you speak English,' said Jeb, 'for I can tell you we mean you no harm and are only travelling northwards through your country.'

The Apache leader stared at Jeb for a few moments before he spoke. 'All white men our enemies, all white men bring harm to Apache,' he said harshly, his lips hardly moving as he spoke. He made a sign to two of his men who laid down their rifles and quickly bound Jeb's and Wade's hands behind their backs. They pushed them roughly to their horses and slung them across the animals' backs. Their ankles were tied tightly and the rope passed under the horses' bellies to link it with that round their wrists. The remaining Indians gathered the white men's saddles and equipment and piled them on the packhorse. The leader shouted an order and the party moved round the rocks to where two more Indians stood with their ponies. Once everyone was mounted the Indians with a whoop of triumph kicked their ponies into a gallop.

For an hour all that Wade saw of the countryside was the dust and scrub which was flashed past immediately below his horse's flying hoofs. He was thankful that the rope underneath the horse had been fastened tightly for he realised if it had not been so he would have slipped round and been battered by the animal's flaying hoofs. His stomach and ribs were battered by the horse's back and he hoped the hard, uncomfortable ride would not be too much for Jeb.

He was thankful when the gallop gradually slackened and then slowed to a walk. He heard shouting and craning his neck upwards he saw they had reached the Indian village. Women and children and old men came to greet them with shouts of pleasure at the sight of prisoners.

The leader of the party which had brought them in produced a knife and with sharp slashes cut the ropes which held Wade and Jeb and the two men slipped from the horses' backs to fall into a heap on the hard ground. The horses were led away to one end of the village by two young boys and the prisoners were ignored as the Indians gathered round the Apache who had led the party.

Wade started to whisper to Jeb but stopped suddenly when he realised by the look which Jeb gave him that he was listening to the Apaches. Wade's heart beat faster; Jeb understood the Apache tongue! The next ten minutes were anxious ones for Wade. He realised there was some sort of debate or argument going on amongst the group of men and he guessed it must be something to do with their fate. He also had time to see that the village consisted of about twenty wickeyups and did not appear to be of a permanent nature.

The group of Indians began to break up and the leader of the party which had captured them walked towards Wade and Jeb. He was followed by four of his band and when they reached the prisoners he stared sullenly at them, his eyes smouldering with anger. Suddenly he spun round and walked away. The four remaining Apaches grabbed Jeb and Wade and dragged them roughly across the hard ground and dumped them outside one of the wickeyups.

When they had gone Wade and Jeb pushed themselves into more comfortable positions with their backs against the wickeyup.

'I didn't know you knew their language,' whispered Wade. 'What was going on over there?'

Jeb mustered a grin. 'I didn't want our charming friend to know I could understand them thet's why I used English when they captured us. Seems this Indian trouble is a series of small outbreaks. It could develop big but thet seems unlikely at the moment. We've been taken by a small group which sent out three raiding parties. The chief's in charge of one and not returned yet. Our friend was all for dealing with us here an' now but most of the others thought they should wait fer the chief to git back; not thet it will make any difference to us. As I see it this Indian doesn't think much of his chief, I figure he reckons he should be their leader.'

'Any hope of the Army ridin' in?' asked Wade hopefully.

Jeb shook his head. 'Not an earthly, son,' he said. 'These Indians will hev lookouts posted an' at the first sign of any opposition they'll move camp; this is no permanent fixture, jest look at these wickeyups they're only of a temporary nature.'

Wade looked round desperately. 'If only we could git free.' He tested the rope which tied his hands but it was unyielding.

'It's no use,' said Jeb. 'Be careful what you do there's a young buck watching us all the time.'

Wade had been surprised that a guard had not been posted near to them but now he realised it wasn't necessary and the Indian had taken up a position on the opposite side of the camp.

'Guess all we can do is hope,' he said dejectedly.

'Thet's right, son,' replied Jeb. 'Something may turn up.' He tried to sound hopeful for the sake of the young cowboy.

The Apaches took no notice of them and as the sun moved higher the heat became more unbearable for the two men lying in the open. They tried to roll round into the slight shadow cast by the wickeyup but a warning shout from the watching Apache stopped them.

It was mid-afternoon when the distant whoops of another returning party brought the Indians running to greet the new arrivals. The yelling grew louder and the waiting Apaches added their own shouts to add to the fearsome noise.

'Guess this lot's also hed a successful time,' observed Jeb sombrely.

Six Indians mounted on powerful ponies rode into camp. Both Jeb and Wade stiffened when they saw the twisting, bouncing forms of two white men dragged by taut ropes behind two galloping horses. With chilling whoops the young Indians brought their ponies to a sliding halt. The two white men rolled on to their backs coughing and spitting trying to get rid of the dust and dirt which had been flung into their mouths as they gasped for breath behind the flying hoofs. Their clothes were ripped and torn and their legs bled from the contact with the rough ground.

'Saunders and Corby!' Wade gasped when he recognised the battered, bloody faces of the two prisoners.

Jeb looked startled. 'They must hev been

tailing us when they were jumped by this lot. Wonder how they knew we had left town?'

The delighted shouts of the Indians were subsiding and Wade was about to speak when he saw Jeb intently trying to pick out something from the chattering. A few minutes passed and Wade looked questioningly at the old prospector.

'Seems no fate is too good fer your ex-partners,' he said grimly. 'Seems they resisted capture and killed two Apaches.'

'Why didn't they kill them there and then?' asked Wade.

'Slow revenge is more to their liking,' explained Jeb.

'Looks as if they've hed a fair amount of punishment already,' said Wade looking at the two men staggering to their feet.

'They'll be all right,' replied Jeb. 'They won't have been dragged very far like thet; the Apaches want them fer greater amusement.'

Wade shuddered at the meaning of the words.

Fear filled the eyes of Saunders and Corby as they swayed at the end of the ropes which still connected them to the horses. They stared wide-eyed at the Indians who surrounded them and mocked them. Suddenly their attention was broken by the fiendish yells and pounding hoofs of the third returning party. The Apaches split and turned to greet a group of eight Indians leading three horses across which were slung three more captives. Wade could not see their faces and he wondered who the poor, unfortunate white men could be. He turned his gaze to the Indian who led the party into camp. He sat tall on his pony; his broad, powerful shoulders topped a lithe, strong body. His features seemed to be less cruel than the Apaches Wade had seen so far. Although dark, his eyes seemed to burn with an intense light and Wade reckoned they could reveal the depths of ferocity or kindness as the mood struck this man.

He swung lightly from the pony's back and from the way the people greeted him with triumphant shouts Wade knew he must be the chief. Turning, he issued instructions to his party and the ropes binding the three men to the horses were slashed allowing them to slip to the hard ground. It was then that Jeb and Wade saw their faces.

'Curt, Red an' Slim,' Jeb gasped. 'They must hev broken out of jail an' were foolish enough to follow us; you see what gold fever does, Wade.'

There was a great feeling of triumph amongst the Apaches at the capture of so many white men in one day. The chief strolled across to Saunders and Corby, eyed them contemptuously for a moment and congratulated the leader of the party which had captured them. He turned and looked around him and Wade saw him seek out the Indian who had surprised them early that same day. The Indian said something and pointed in the direction of Jeb and Wade and then the two Apaches walked towards them. The chief was staring at them as he moved closer. Suddenly, when he was about five yards from them, he stopped. Wade saw his eyes widen and beside him he heard Jeb gasp sharply.

'Chief Neva!' The words escaped from Jeb's tight lips.

'Carter, The Little One!' The Indian was equally surprised. He turned quickly and spoke sharply to an Indian behind him. The man moved forward swiftly and pulled out a knife. For one brief moment Wade thought this was the end. The knife flashed twice and the ropes which bound Jeb fell to the ground.

As he pushed himself to his feet he half turned to Wade. 'There's hope, son,' he whispered. He straightened and faced the chief.

Their captor was protesting loudly to his chief and Wade noticed the cruel line of frustration which had come across the mouth of the man who had designs on the chieftainship. He spoke in English to make sure Jeb could understand.

'Why release this man, Neva?'

'This man goes free, Running Dog,' answered Neva. 'He must come to no harm with my people for he once saved the life of their chief.'

'Your life, Neva?' asked Running Dog.

The chief nodded. 'It was many moons ago when I was young and for that he must be released.'

'Let one white man go and you may as well release them all,' scorned Running Dog. 'Our efforts will all come to nought.'

'What difference will one life make? Carter, The Little One will not harm us,' answered Neva quietly.

'He is my prisoner,' snapped Running Dog, 'and I demand his life.'

'This man will go free,' replied Neva firmly.

'Is our chief getting soft?' Running Dog spoke contemptuously. 'If so it is time for a stronger man to be chief.'

Neva stiffened, raising himself to his full height. 'You speak with a wicked tongue,

Running Dog. My orders are that he should be released and not be molested by my people again.'

Running Dog was not to be outdone. 'Maybe Carter's presence in this country is harmful to the Apache,' he shouted. 'I say you should question why he is here.'

The chief realised he was in a position from which he could not turn; it was a reasonable request and a murmur of agreement came from the other Apaches.

'Very well,' answered Neva. 'I will grant that wish but I will be the judge. If his presence is of harm to my people he will be escorted back to the white man's land. Come, Carter.' He spun on his heels and the Indians made way for him. Jeb followed him without even a backward glance at Wade who had watched the whole proceedings with an anxious mind.

He saw anger and hatred smouldering in the deep sunken eyes of Running Dog as he stared after his chief. Wade's gaze passed beyond the Indian and he saw the captives being roughly handled, dragged and pushed in his direction. As they were sent tumbling beside him Wade saw fear in all their eyes.

'So they got you too,' said Saunders huskily. 'A lot of good your gold will do you now.'

'None of you need have followed,' replied Wade. 'Your greed got you into this.'

'It's all right fer you to preach,' snarled Curt Mason, 'You'll soon be out of here.'

'The same way as you most likely,' answered Wade.

'What? With Carter well in with these savages,' snapped Red. 'He's spent so much time out here he's almost one of them; look at the way the chief's treating him. You've no worry, he'll soon have you free.'

'Maybe you too,' mused Wade as he stared at the chief's wickeyup wondering what was going on inside.

TWELVE

When Chief Neva entered his wickeyup he turned to face Jeb before seating himself cross-legged on the floor. Jeb waited until the chief had settled himself then he took up a similar position opposite the chief and waited for the Apache to speak first.

'My old friend, it is a bad time to be in these parts,' said Neva quietly. 'Why are you here?'

Jeb stared at the chief thoughtfully for a moment and decided that his best course was to tell the chief the truth. He related quickly the essential parts of the story since his meeting with Wade and their reason for being in this part of Arizona. As the story unfolded the Indian's face grew serious and he looked hard at the old man.

'I know of that gold,' he said, 'but I did not want it to be revealed. I feel that if the white man gets to know, there will be another Black Hills and a worse tragedy than we are suffering now will come to the Apache nation just as it did to our brothers the Sioux. An invasion by the white man on that scale would spell final doom to the Apache nation. I ask you to forget this venture.

'I know your words are true,' replied Jeb, 'but my friend an' I had definitely agreed to keep this a secret from all white men. He seeks the gold for a special purpose; I ask you to hear that story from himself.'

Neva called to the Apache on guard at the entrance to the wickeyup and when he appeared inside the chief issued an order briefly. The man hurried away and a few moments later returned with Wade. When the young man's eyes were accustomed to the light inside the dwelling he saw Neva

130

indicate to him to sit down beside Jeb.

'I have told the chief why we are travelling through this country,' said Jeb. 'Now he wants to hear from you why we seek this gold.'

Wade looked hard at the Indian. He had a feeling that this was a man who understood straight talk. The dignity of the Indian impressed Wade and he realised this was a man to whom he could not lie.

'I mean the Apache no harm,' explained Wade slowly but convincingly. 'I wish to find the gold to help the Mexican family who discovered the mine.'

'You mean Manuel Cordoba?' asked the chief with some surprise.

Wade was astonished at the question. 'Yes,' he replied. 'You know *Señor* Cordoba?'

'I do, but go on with your story,' instructed Neva.

'Bad times are facing the Cordoba's,' went on Wade. He saw a look of doubt flash in the eyes of the usually impassive face. He realised the Indian must think the Cordobas rich after their discovery of the gold. '*Señor* Manuel Cordoba used a lot of money to try to discover his brother who returned to this country; he also used much to help his people and the ranch he bought had suffered badly from drought.'

'Manuel's brother died at the hands of white men greedy for gold. We buried him near the mountain and caught the killers. Why did not Manuel or one of his family come?' he added thoughtfully.

'He is an old man now and he refused to let his family come, saying that Superstition Mountain is nothing but evil. He tried hard to stop me from coming but I owe them a debt for saving my life,' Wade explained.

'I can vouch that all this is true,' put in Jeb.

'If my old friend believes then so do I but also I can tell this young man does not speak with a forked tongue,' said Neva.

A sense of relief flowed through Wade and he felt some of the tension go out of his body although he knew that all was not settled.

'Carter, The Little One, tells me that you intended to keep this a secret,' said Neva. Wade nodded. 'Then why are those men following you?' The Indian's tongue was like a whip probing some flaw in the story.

Wade stiffened but Jeb spoke quickly.

'Two of them were trailing my friend to kill him,' he explained. 'They arrived at the Cordoba ranch and recognised Cordoba, intended to steal the map but Wade took it first. Since then they have left him alive hoping he would lead them to the gold. The others unfortunately overheard about the map when we were in Tombstone but I assure you they are the only ones who know.'

'Then when they have been dealt with you will be the only ones and the secret will be safe again,' said Neva. 'You will be released and leave this camp immediately to help Manuel Cordoba.'

Wade's eyes brightened. He was about to thank the chief when Jeb spoke.

'We are grateful, Neva,' he said. 'But tell me one thing; why was there no great invasion of white men after the Cordobas discovered the gold?'

'The mine remained only a rumour after they left,' replied the chief, 'and not many white men would move through Apache country on the strength of a rumour. The Cordobas and my father were great friends and they saw that if the presence of gold was made known it would be the death of the Apache. They agreed to keep it a secret.'

'As we too will keep it a secret,' said Wade seriously, 'knowing the friendship between your father and *Señor* Manuel.'

Chief Neva stood up putting an end to the conversation. The two white men pushed themselves to their feet and followed the chief from the wickeyup.

When Running Dog watched his chief lead the white man to the wickeyup he was filled with anger and hatred. He expected Neva to allow his captives to go free but he felt that his chief should have heard the white men in front of the tribe; he had no witnesses to know what the white man had said.

Running Dog mingled with the other Apaches and then gradually worked his way to the back of the chief's wickeyup where he knelt with ear pressed close to the wall of the shelter. His thoughts raced and his anger rose when he heard the talk of gold and realised that Neva had kept the information to himself and not used it to benefit the Apache.

When he realised the discussion was almost over he sneaked away from the wickeyup and sought out his close friend, Swift Bullet. He drew him to one side and quickly told him what he had overheard.

'Neva has failed in his duty to the Apache,' Running Dog insisted. 'He is going to let these two white men go. We will follow them and seize the gold. It will put us on equal terms with the white man and with that power we can be great amongst the Apache nation.' Running Dog's eyes gleamed with his thirst for power. 'Neva will be looked down upon because he did not use the knowledge of the gold and we will be great.'

'But the white men will come in thousands after the yellow metal,' pointed out Swift Bullet. 'He will over-run the Apache land.'

'Not if we are ready for him and stand firm,' insisted Running Dog. 'He will have to seek our terms and that will make us great with our people.'

'If we leave now we will be missed at tomorrow's ceremonies when the white men die,' said Swift Bullet.

'We need not leave until the white men are dead,' replied Running Dog. 'The trail will be easy to find; I know they are heading for Superstition Mountain.'

Swift Bullet gasped; his eyes filled with horror. 'I cannot go to Superstition Mountain,' he stuttered. 'It is full of evil spirits who turned the Pimas to stone.'

'Tales!' hissed Running Dog angrily. 'You must come or I will kill you now you know about the gold!' His eyes burned fiercely and Swift Bullet knew that he would carry out his threat if necessary.

'But the same fate might befall us,' Swift

Bullet protested weakly.

Running Dog spat contemptuously. 'Are you afraid? You are not worthy to be an Apache.' His hand fell to his knife but before he could draw it Swift Bullet stopped him.

'I will come,' he said. 'I will try to appease the spirits with some offering.'

'Forget the stories,' advised Running Dog. 'If the gold is going to bring us the power we want we can ignore them. The spirits will be pleased that we use the gold for the benefit of the Apache and by having it keep the white man from the mountain home of the spirits.'

There was a shout from the far side of the camp and Running Dog suddenly realised the chief wanted him. He ran quickly and saw Neva standing with Jeb and Wade whilst an Indian brought their horses.

'Your two prisoners are to go free,' said Neva. 'They mean no harm to the Apache and they must travel unharmed through our country.'

Running Dog's eyes darkened as he faced his chief. 'I do not like this,' he said between tight lips. 'You are weak to fall for the tales of a white man. Remember this, if anything goes wrong you will have to answer your people.' He turned and strode swiftly away.

Neva watched him for a moment before

turning to Wade and Jeb. 'Don't worry,' he said. 'He is angry now but he will be all right tomorrow when he wreaks some of his revenge on the white man.'

Wade glanced at the five men who were still lying beside the wickeyup and, although they were his enemies, he felt horror in his heart that they were to be left to the fearsome Apache tortures.

'It will be well if you ride now.' Neva's words broke into Wade's thoughts.

The two men took the reins from the Indian, and swung into the saddles and pushed their horses forward.

'Wade, what about us?'

'Don't leave us here, Jeb!'

'Save us from these savages!'

Cries of alarm came from the five men when they saw Wade and Jeb swing into the saddles. Fear rang in their voices which resounded in Wade's ears as he rode out of the Indian camp. The anguish in the shouts haunted him with every yard they moved.

'Jeb, we can't leave them there!' Wade broke the silence after they had ridden a mile.

The old man looked shrewdly at his companion. 'I knew it was troublin' you,' he said. 'Thought I'd let you fight it out fer yourself. I'm sorry thet side won an' you see it thet way.'

'We must go back and help them,' cried Wade.

'Thet's impossible, son,' answered Jeb sharply.

'We can't leave white men to the Apaches tortures,' snapped Wade.

Jeb looked seriously at Wade. 'Son, you don't know what you're sayin'. We'd be lucky if we got near them.'

'Darkness could hide our movements,' put in Wade.

'Maybe,' answered Jeb, 'but supposin' we managed it; every Apache would be after our blood, our chance of gettin' to Superstition Mountain would be practically nil. What about the Cordobas?'

'They wouldn't want me to leave men to torture because of the gold,' replied Wade. 'Maybe Manuel was right and the mountain is evil and this is the result.'

'You'd sacrifice saving the Cordobas from ruin to rescue those worthless coyotes. You realize they'd thank you with one breath an' then kill you fer the map. The gold fever's in them, son, there's nothing they wouldn't do to get it even if you saved their lives.'

'Thet's a chance I'd have to take,' said Wade. He turned his horse but Jeb laid a restraining hand on the reins. He looked hard at the young cowboy.

'I've always reckoned you a man of honour,' he said seriously. 'Think of Chief Neva. You gave your word. If you rescue these men you'll break thet word. The chief trusts you. You heard Running Dog say he would hold Neva responsible should anything happen because of our release. This would be just what he wanted; Neva would be disgraced and Running Dog could seize power in the tribe.'

Wade shook his head. 'I know,' he said quietly. 'I hate doing it, for the chief's sake, but I can't leave white men to the mercy of those savages.'

'Be careful of thet word,' snapped Jeb angrily. 'They are no worse than those white men, they deserve to die.'

'Maybe it is what they deserve,' agreed Wade. 'A swift death would be one thing but slow torture is another. I can't see them left there.'

Jeb saw it was useless to argue any more. 'All right,' he said, 'we'll find a little hollow an' camp until dark.'

They found a suitable place a short distance away and once they had settled down Jeb renewed his efforts to persuade Wade to give up his idea but Wade was adamant. At the end of an hour the old man shrugged his shoulders.

'You're makin' a big mistake,' he said, 'but once again I can't see you face it alone.'

'Thanks,' replied Wade, his voice full of appreciation for Jeb's support.

THIRTEEN

Darkness was spreading across the Arizona countryside when the two men moved out of the hollow. They led their horses to a group of rocks about a quarter of a mile from the Indian encampment. After securing their horses Jeb motioned to Wade to sit down.

'What are we waiting for?' asked the young cowboy. He was tensed up to the task ahead and now a further wait would only add to the anxiety. He marvelled at the outward calmness of the older man.

'All is still quiet,' replied Jeb. 'There will be certain ceremonies tonight; they will bewail the loss of their men and follow it with an excited anticipation of vengeance to be wrought on their captives tomorrow.'

'But surely it would be better to go whilst it's quiet,' said Wade.

Jeb smiled. 'When the ceremonies are at their height everyone's attention will be occupied, then we move in.'

Wade nodded realising the wisdom of the old man's words.

Half an hour passed before Jeb signalled to Wade to follow him and when they moved from behind the rocks they saw the glow of huge fires in the encampment. The two men crept stealthily forward and when they neared the camp they dropped on to their stomachs and crept Indian fashion to a vantage point behind some boulders. They peered round them cautiously; the leaping flares cast an eerie glow across the whole en-campment. Indians were gathering in a huge circle around the fires. The men were naked except for a breech-clout and their dark bodies shone in the light of the flames. Suddenly a yell pierced the night air followed by low wailing and chanting. Wade shuddered.

'The Song of Death,' whispered Jeb.

His words reminded Wade of the real pur-pose for their return. He tore his eyes away from the fascinating, weird scene and glanced towards the wickeyup outside of which he had last seen the prisoners.

'They are not there!' he gasped.

'I know,' replied Jeb. 'I noticed that as soon as we arrived here.'

'What do we do now?' asked Wade seeing failure looming in his face.

'More than likely they'll be inside thet wickeyup,' answered Jeb. 'It would be the most convenient to put them in.'

'What did the Indians want to put them inside for?' said Wade. 'I thought being out-side…'

'There's more mental torture in listening to thet wailing and not being able to see what is goin' on than to be outside and see it all,' cut in Jeb whose eyes had been meticulously searching the camp all the time. 'There's no one movin' about,' he went on, 'we'll make our play whilst all of them are occupied out there.'

He glided silently away to the left and Wade followed, keeping close behind Jeb. Slowly they worked their way round towards the wickeyup which they had marked out as being the one which possibly held the captives. Wade was thankful that the flames had died a little leaving the outer parts of the camp on the edge of darkness. Suddenly the chanting stopped and both men froze in their tracks. Wade glanced anxiously at Jeb who was watching the Apaches carefully. The young cowboy shuddered; the sudden cessation of noise left behind a ghostly penetrating silence. As suddenly as it had stopped a shriek rose skywards and the chanting began in earnest again in a much quicker tempo than before.

Jeb tapped his young partner and moved forward quickly but silently. Once behind the wickeyup they paused before edging their way slowly round the side. They hesitated again on the edge of the shadow of the hut. Jeb carefully examined the camp and satisfied that everyone's attention was riveted on the centre of the encampment he moved swiftly to the doorway and entered the wickeyup with Wade close on his heels. The old man was tense and ready with knife drawn in case a guard had been posted inside the shelter but he was relieved when in spite of the gloom he could see only the huddled forms of the captives lying on the floor.

'We're in luck,' he whispered to Wade. 'The right hut and no guard. Work fast in case someone spotted us.'

Wade glanced quickly through the doorway. 'No one coming,' he said and the two men dropped on their knees beside the five startled men.

As his knife flashed cleanly through the ropes Jeb whispered urgently. 'Don't rush it when you're free,' he said. 'You're mighty lucky Wade insisted on comin' back; I'd hev let you rot. Wade an' I go first, then it's every man fer himself but take my tip, leave one at a time; a sudden rush would be spotted.'

The five men who had spent a miserable time with their thoughts since they had been dumped in the wickeyup scrambled to their feet mumbling their thanks.

'Got a gun?' asked Corby.

'Yes, but not for you,' answered Wade. 'We've given you a chance, now you're on your own.'

He pushed Jeb forward and the two friends crouched low, hugging the side of the wickey-up as they glided to the darkness. Once they reached the shelter of some boulders they breathed more freely. The weird chanting still rose on the night air as they made their way to their horses. They had reached them when a sound to their left froze them in their tracks. They laid comforting hands on their horses to keep them quiet. Shrieks and yells came distinctly from the encampment but it was the voice close at hand which held Wade's attention.

'We've lost them, but they can't be far

away an' they must hev horses; if only we could jump them...' Wade stiffened when he recognised Corby's voice. His hand moved to his Colt and Jeb, detecting the movement even in the darkness, laid a restraining hand on the young cowboy.

They heard the scraping of feet on a rock and then all was silent. Jeb waited a few moments before swinging on to his horse and taking the reins of the pack horse led it away. Wade climbed into the saddle and kept close to Jeb who held as fast a pace as the darkness would allow.

The rising sun was breaking the horizon when Chief Neva ordered the white men to be brought from the wickeyup. Three Apaches hurried from the gathering to the hut but immediately reappeared yelling at the top of their voices that the prisoners had escaped. The whole tribe stared at them in amazement as the truth was confirmed by the severed ropes held by one of the men.

Running Dog, equally shocked, was not slow to seize the chance offered to him. He leaped to his feet, snatched the ropes from the man's hand and turned to face his chief. His eyes smouldered with anger and hate as he held out the ropes at arm's length.

'It is Neva's fault that these men have escaped,' he yelled. 'See, the ropes have been cut with a knife; the two men whom Neva freed must have returned and set our prisoners free!'

Neva drew himself to his full height as he impassively faced his accuser. 'You speak with false tongue, Running Dog,' he said. His voice was quiet but powerful. 'Carter, The Little One, nor his friend would break their word given to Neva.'

'Who else could have freed them?' screamed Running Dog.

There was a murmur amongst the Indians and they all looked at their chief for his answer.

'I know not,' replied Neva.

'No one else could,' laughed Running Dog scornfully. 'You believe only what your heart wants you to believe. You will not face the truth.'

'And you do not know the truth,' replied Neva.

'I believe what my mind tells me is the only answer,' shouted Running Dog. 'A man who is ruled by his heart is not fit to be chief.'

There was a murmur of approval amongst the Indians and Running Dog, sensing the feeling of the gathering, seized his chance before Neva could speak. He strode around the circle of Apaches displaying his powerful body as he screamed insults at his chief.

'Neva is no longer the mighty warrior. His prowess on the battlefield is marred by his faintheartedness in camp when dealing with white men. The chief must always be powerful and not turn from his duty even though it means heartaches for him. Neva spared his feelings when he let the white men go and now they return to set the others free to do us harm.' Running Dog saw that he held the gathering in his hand and he was determined not to let Neva speak again. His voice started to rise as he swore vengeance on the white men and on his chief. 'How will he treat white men in the future? The time will come when he will spare them even on the field of battle. I say he is no longer fit to lead us, he should pay for his weakness and someone else should rule in his place!'

The Apaches were lashed into a fury by Running Dog's tongue, screamed their approval and cried shame upon Neva. Immediately Swift Bullet called out Running Dog's name and soon all the Indians were shouting it. Running Dog smiled to himself but his face was masked with contempt for Neva. He moved quickly to the side of the chief.

'Even your people see the wrong of your ways, you must bow to their wishes.' Running Dog's tongue was like a lash as he stared at Neva, mockery and hate in his dark, deep-set eyes. 'They want a man who will be strong in his dealings with the white men,' he went on.

'Like Running Dog?' put in Neva contemptuously. 'You will be no good for them, you act without thinking and that means trouble. You…'

'You are not wanted,' screamed Running Dog. 'Go before it is too late.' The Indians took up the cry, calling for Neva to go.

He looked round his people slowly as they jeered at him. 'I will go,' he called loudly, 'as you wish it, but I will return with the two white men.'

'Unless we find them first,' answered Running Dog. Using his new-found authority he ordered search parties to be formed quickly and immediately the whole encampment became a place of great activity and Neva was forgotten as he made his way slowly to his wickeyup. As he gathered his rifle and knife and prepared for the trail he heard the preparations going on outside. Suddenly the air was rent by ear-splitting yells and the thunder of hoofs as the parties left the camp.

When the pound of the ponies faded in the distance Neva walked from his wickey-up. He paused at the entrance gazing sadly round the encampment deserted except for the squaws, children and old men. No one took any notice of him. He realised he had not put up much resistance to Running Dog but he knew it was useless under the circumstances. He had no evidence to disprove Running Dog's theories and even in his own mind Neva had to admit that it seemed more than likely that the rescue had been carried out by Carter and O'Hara. Sadly he walked to his pony, patted it affectionately on the neck, climbed on to its back and sent it into a trot away from the camp in the direction of Superstition Mountain.

It was with mixed feelings that Jake Saunders and Pete Corby watched daylight spreading across the Arizona countryside as they stumbled through the scrub. Once they had realised that their plan to take the horses from Jeb and Wade would not materialise they had determined to put as much ground between them and the Indians before daylight. Now a day full of potential danger stared them in the face.

'What are we going to do, Jake?' asked Pete wearily. 'We've got to find a place to rest; we can't keep goin' all day an' those savages will soon be searchin' for us.'

'There's no place to hide yet,' mumbled Jake hoarsely. 'We've got to keep goin'.'

Soon the heat of the sun was beginning to beat into the two weary men who kept glancing behind them, a look of expected doom in their eyes. Suddenly Jake grabbed Pete's arm.

'There's a drop ahead of us,' he said, his words croaking from a dried throat. 'Maybe we'll find some place for shelter.'

From somewhere they found new energy and as they hurried forward they began to see the depression ahead of them was bigger than they had first thought. They pulled up on the edge of a six foot drop and hung on to each other as their legs started to buckle. Their eyes widened in amazement, they turned their heads to stare at each other, excitement shone in their eyes as grins split their faces. With a sudden yell they jumped down the six feet and started to run down the steady slope which formed one side of a dry valley two hundred feet below. As they ran they yelled as loud as they could and waved their arms and battered sombreros. Some measure of relief crossed them when they saw the covered wagon drawn by four mules, which had been the cause of their first excitement, pull to a halt.

One man jumped down from the wagon and faced Saunders and Corby with a rifle, whilst the other stayed on the seat holding the mules under control.

'Know them, pa?' the man with the rifle called over his shoulder.

'Nope,' came the answer. 'Fools to be out here without horses an' guns,' he muttered to himself.

Saunders and Corby, gasping for breath, stopped in front of the younger man who stared hard at them. They swayed on their feet, laughing deep in their throats as they fought for words in their excitement.

'We're sure mighty glad to see you,' panted Saunders.

'What's happened to you two?' queried the young man motioning towards the wagon with his rifle. 'Don't you know the Apaches are on the war-path?'

The two men stumbled to the wagon and found some relief leaning on the huge wheels.

'We escaped from them last night!' answered Saunders.

The young man stared at them incredulously and Corby, seeing the doubt in the man's eyes, held his wrists out to reveal the marks of the ropes. 'Thet's how we lost our horses an' guns,' he said to emphasise Jake's statement.

The old man jumped down from the wagon and handed a canteen of water to Saunders who, after having a drink, passed it to Corby. Saunders wiped a hairy hand across his lips. 'Thanks,' he said. 'We'd appreciate some help.'

'Sure,' nodded the older man. 'Git in the wagon we're headin' out of this goddamned country.'

'Wal, we weren't figurin' on leavin' if at all possible,' answered Saunders. 'I know things looked black fer us but now we've found you I think we can help our friends.'

'Friends?' said the young man curiously.

'We left them near Superstition Mountain,' lied Saunders. 'We were headin' for Tombstone fer supplies when the Indians jumped us, our friends know nothing of the trouble. If you could let us have some food an' water an' two of those three horses you've got tied to the back of the wagon we'd ride back an' warn them.'

The young man looked at his father, who nodded and soon Saunders and Corby were fixed up with mounts, food and water.

'You're mighty lucky to have met up with us,' said the older man. 'We've been out here a long while prospectin' and we always carry a lot of equipment with us, sure we can fix you up with a couple of Colts.'

The two men showed their appreciation, wished the two prospectors luck and turned their horses in the direction of Superstition Mountain.

Jeb Carter and Wade O'Hara kept to a steady pace throughout the night and Wade followed the older man without question. Jeb led the way south before circling northwards hoping to mislead the Apaches when they started their hunt. The result was that they were not as far north of the encampment as Wade would have liked by daybreak.

'I reckon we'll keep pushin' on fer awhile,' said Jeb as the sun broke the horizon. 'Those Apaches will soon be searchin' fer us.'

It was not until the heat was becoming unpleasant that Jeb called a halt amongst a group of boulders at the top of a ridge.

'Well git a good view from up here without being seen an' will get plenty of warning should trouble be headin' our way,' observed Jeb as they dismounted.

Wade made the horses as comfortable as possible whilst leaving them ready for immediate action should it be necessary. The two men had something to eat and Wade insisted on taking the first watch whilst Jeb got some rest.

As Jeb settled down Wade got his spyglass from his saddlebag, climbed higher amongst the boulders and surveyed the countryside. Suddenly he stiffened with surprise and steadied his spyglass on an old hut about three miles away. He watched carefully for a few minutes before he called to Jeb who scrambled to his feet quickly and was soon beside Wade.

'Hut over there,' said Wade and handed the spyglass to Jeb who grunted and trained it on the hut.

'Seen anyone?' asked Jeb.

'One old man who seems to be preparing to leave,' answered Wade.

'Got him,' answered Jeb. 'Just brought some packs out of the hut. Must be a prospector an' got wind of the Indian trouble.'

The two men watched him for a while then suddenly Wade grasped Jeb's arm. 'Look along there,' he said and indicated the ridge to their left.

Three figures on foot had appeared on the

edge and Jeb turned the spyglass on them. 'Curt Mason, Red an' Slim,' gasped Jeb. 'They're lucky to hev kept alive so far.'

The three men started down the long slope towards the hut unaware that they were under close observation.

'Reckon we're in luck,' said Curt as he urged his two weary companions onwards. 'There are two horses in front maybe some more round the back.'

'Hope so,' muttered Red. 'We'll give those devils the slip yet.'

They were near the hut before the old prospector came out carrying another bundle. He stopped with surprise when he saw the three sweating, leg-weary men approaching. He eyed them suspiciously and weighed them up with one glance. 'Roughnecks,' he muttered to himself. Aloud he said: 'What happened to you three, surprised you ain't got horses?'

'Indians got them,' answered Curt as they stopped close to the old man. 'We were lucky to git away. Got any mounts we can hev to git out of this hole?'

'Sorry,' replied the prospector, 'only got those two, need 'em both. Can give you food an' water though.'

'Can't ride out on them!' snapped Curt. His eyes narrowed, his face darkened as he looked hard at the old man still holding the bundle.

'Sorry but thet's all I hev...' The words were choked in the old man's throat as Curt grabbed him by the neck.

There was a mad gleam in Mason's eyes, his grip tightened. The prospector dropped his bundle but before his hand could reach for his gun Red and Slim grabbed his arms. His eyes widened, there was a struggle for breath, then suddenly he went limp. Curt released his grip, stepped round Slim and jumped to the doorway against the side of which he had seen a rifle. He grabbed it and swung round to face Red and Slim who let the old man fall to the floor.

'Wal,' he said, grinning all over his face, 'There are two horses, I take one, who takes the other?'

The two men stared at him for a moment.

'Guess we'll take it in turns one up and two up,' answered Red wondering what Curt was getting at.

'Not me,' replied Curt. 'I ain't bein' slowed up fer anyone. You ride two up if you like but I ain't waitin' fer you. Those red savages will be ridin' hard after us an' a horse with two up won't outrun the Indian ponies.'

The two men stared at Curt incredulously

then suddenly the realisation of his words struck them. As one man they looked down at the body of the old prospector, saw his gun and dived for it. Slim was faster but his fingers had only touched the butt when he felt a vice-like grip on his wrist. With a sharp jerk Red twisted Slim over and fell on top of him. He smashed his fist into Slim's face and with one movement flung himself over and jerked the gun from its holster.

Curt laughed raucously when he saw the frenzied terror of a fight for survival, then turned and walked into the hut to look for food.

As the gun came from the leather Slim pushed himself from the ground hurling himself at Red. The crash of bodies sent the two men rolling in the dust and the gun was flung from Red's grasp. Slim jerked himself over and dived full length towards the gun only to be pulled up short by Red's iron grip on his left ankle. Red clung to Slim as he stretched his fingers trying desperately to cover the few remaining inches to the gun. He could feel Red struggling to his knees, whilst maintaining the grip on his ankle. Suddenly Slim twisted over sharply and catching Red unawares flung him over on to his back so that he lost the hold on Slim. Slim scrambled round and fell on his knees beside the gun. His eyes wide with triumph he grabbed the weapon and still on his knees turned to see Red leaping at him. He squeezed the trigger, saw Red jerk under the impact of the bullet but the forward momentum brought the body crashing against him. The gun fell from his grasp as he rolled over on to his face. He saw Red fall beside him and lay still. Panting for breath he pushed himself slowly to his knees, his eyes riveted on the gun which to him meant survival. He leaned forward to take it but froze with his hand still above the gun. A shadow had fallen across the weapon!

Slowly he raised his head to see Running Dog gazing impassively down at him. Slim recoiled with horror. His desperate fight had been in vain. Suddenly he was galvanised into action which was born out of terror. He fell forward snatching at the gun but his fingers had not touched it when Running Dog's rifle broke the silence. Slim jerked and twisted as the lead crashed into him sending him sprawling into death beside Red. Running Dog turned and signalled to the two Apaches standing close to the wall on either side of the doorway of the hut.

Inside the shelter Curt had found some

food and was busy gathering it together when he heard the first shot. He laughed to himself. 'Who rides with me?' he shouted. There was no answer then a second shot resounded in the hut. Curt frowned; puzzled he walked to the doorway, stepped outside and froze in his tracks when he saw Running Dog and six other Apaches. In desperation he jerked his rifle upwards but before he could squeeze the trigger he found himself in the unfriendly grip of the two Apaches who had been waiting for his appearance. Curt struggled but it was useless and soon his hands were tied behind his back and he was flung across one of the old prospector's horses.

Running Dog ordered his followers to return to camp whilst he and Swift Bullet tracked down the other white men. The Apaches rode off with triumphant shrieks and Running Dog and Swift Bullet watched them go before walking to their ponies.

'The other white men will be found at Superstition Mountain, we will let them lead us to the gold!' said Running Dog.

FOURTEEN

Wade and Jeb witnessed the killings with a mixed sense of horror and frustration. When Wade saw Curt attack the old man he automatically jumped to his feet but Jeb grabbed him and pulled him down roughly.

'We'd be too late,' he said. 'Besides, look over there.' He pointed to the rock-strewn rise behind the shack and handed the spyglass to Wade.

Wade focused the spyglass and stiffened when he saw nine Apaches making their way carefully down the slope towards the hut.

'Let's hope they didn't see you,' said Jeb.

Wade looked desperately at Jeb. 'We've got to do something about them,' he said.

'There's nothin' we can do,' replied Jeb sharply. 'If we try anythin' we'll end up back at the Apache camp, tied upside down with our heads roasting over a fire! It's useless to try to help them now. They'll only get what they deserve after their treatment of that old prospector.'

Wade shrugged his shoulders. He knew Jeb

was right. He settled down again amongst the boulders and the two friends watched the events unfold without speaking. When Jeb saw the Apaches ride away he felt some measure of relief.

'At least we're free from thet lot,' he said, 'but there'll be others about so we'll hev to keep our eyes open. Wonder what those other two are up to.' They watched Running Dog and Swift Bullet disappear over the rise behind the hut.

It was an uneasy rest until the middle of the afternoon when Jeb decided it was time to be moving again. They kept to a steady pace, using what cover they could and keeping a careful watch for any signs of Indians but fortunately they saw none.

Two days later, after crossing the Gila, Superstition Mountain came in sight and as they moved across the desert scrubland Wade noticed the change in the landscape and he was amazed at the beauty which he thought could never belong to the desert. Instead of an expanse of bare rock and dust, boulders and uninteresting scrub there now appeared an increasing number of gorgeous plants and shrubs of most unusual kinds. Dominating them all was the saguaro cactus in all its various stages of growth.

'Never seen anythin' like this before, hev you?' smiled Jeb amused by Wade's expression. 'Those little ones about four inches high will be about ten years old and those big ones, some of them fifty feet I reckon, will be more than a hundred.'

They threaded their way onwards with Superstition Mountain growing bigger with every step. The huge block of land seemed to spring from the desert floor. It rose sharply with a few outcrops of rounded hills dropping more gently to the plain. The top for the most part appeared flat, with precipitous cliffs forming the edge in many parts. Towards one end of the plateau there was an additional rise almost as if the mountain had a wart. It had a fascination for Wade and he found something awe-inspiring about this desert mountain.

Jeb swung more to his right towards that part of the mountain which sloped more gently to the desert and when they reached the beginning of the rise he decided to camp and make the climb the next day when they had the full day before them.

'Will we be able to get the horses up?' asked Wade when they were enjoying their meal.

Jeb nodded. 'If we take it steady and watch our step.'

162

'What's that lighter mark?' queried Wade indicating a light streak which ran horizontally in the rock face.

'Thet's supposed to mark the height of the flood,' explained Jeb. He smiled when he saw the puzzled look on Wade's face and went on to enlighten him. 'Superstition gets its name from an old Pima legend which says that in the great flood Indians sought refuge on the mountain. They were told that they must not make any sound until the waters receded. They disobeyed and were immediately turned into stone and you will find on top of the mountain rock shapes which resemble human figures. The Indians say that they are the people who disobeyed. The Spaniards called the mountain Sierra de Espuma so you see why Manuel Cordoba called his ranch by that name.'

The following morning they were up early and after a quick breakfast they started their ascent of the mountain. Remembering tracks from a previous visit Jeb led the way unerringly but, thinking of the horses, he kept to a pace which, although he did not know it, helped those who hoped O'Hara and Carter would lead them to their fortunes.

Although there was considerable daylight left when they reached the top of the moun-

163

tain Carter decided to set up camp for the night. He did not want to push the horses too hard and the climb had not been easy. A feeling that they were being watched had grown upon him but he kept his uneasiness to himself and thought it best to save the horses in case they were needed in a hurry.

When the two men had settled down they studied the Cordoba map and decided that tomorrow they would have to cross the plateau to the cliff-like face of the hill at the other end.

It was a hot ride and took the best part of the day. Jeb kept careful watch but saw signs of no one. He tried to shake off the uneasy feeling but could not do so.

'You're a bit jumpy, Jeb,' observed Wade as they neared the wall of rock.

'Guess thet's Superstition Mountain fer you,' replied Jeb with a hollow laugh.

'Felt it myself,' said Wade, 'but didn't want to say anything. Reckon it's those rocks,' he added nodding towards a line of eroded rocks to the right. 'It sure looks as if there's something in thet Indian legend.'

Jeb grunted and rode on until they were close to the cliff-face. He studied the map and decided they should be half-a-mile to the right. They moved carefully, picking their way round huge rocks which had fallen from the precipitous cliffs leaving a huge area of fantastic upheaval.

After they had organised their camp in a small hollow encircled by huge boulders the two men decided there was still time to make a preliminary investigation of the cliff-face. They made their way out of the hollow to a point close to the huge wall of rock indicated by the map. As they approached this point Wade stopped Jeb.

'The map must be wrong,' he said. 'This is nothing but solid rock and the map seemed to show some way through it.'

'Don't be in too big a hurry,' replied Jeb. 'This may not be accurate to half a mile or so. The Cordobas probably only estimated distance. C'm on, keep lookin'.'

They moved closer to the rock-face and worked their way slowly along. At first they were met by blank cliff walls but gradually these became broken by fissures.

Wade and Jeb continued their way for another quarter of a mile when Jeb stopped.

'You know, Wade,' he said, 'we may not be examinin' these clefts sufficiently, may be the track indicated on the map starts in one of them.'

'You could be right,' said Wade excitedly.

'I've been expecting a fairly wide opening.'

The two men fell to examining every crack in the cliff-face more carefully but success was not easily come by and Jeb was beginning to think they had better give up until tomorrow when Wade, who was about a hundred yards away, suddenly shouted.

'Looks as if I've got something here,' he called.

The old man hurried forward and Wade pointed to a huge cut which ran the full height of the cliff-face.

'This could easily be it,' said Jeb excitedly.

'Not so fast,' answered Wade. 'I've been in a couple of yards and there appears to be a wall of rock but I reckon it bears closer inspection.'

Jeb led the way and found the wall of rock as described by Wade but when Jeb examined it carefully he found that the crack turned to the right and then a few yards further on to the left again. They squeezed their way along and soon realised that the cleft was widening. It still ran the full height of the cliff and allowed an ever increasing amount of light to filter to the bottom. Soon the two men were able to walk side by side and after they had gone a quarter of a mile they realised that a short distance ahead a wall of rock the full height of the cliffs barred their path.

'Looks as if we are coming to a dead-end,' observed Wade.

Jeb did not reply but kept on and a few moments later gasped with surprise when they found themselves on the edge of a shallow bowl about a hundred yards across and bound on all sides by precipitous cliffs the sheerness of which was almost frightening. There was an eeriness about the shaft of light which seemed to plunge straight down to illuminate the bowl. Both men shivered. Jeb pulled out the map and traced the path with his finger.

'I reckon this is it,' he said.

'There's no sign of a mine that I can see,' said Wade.

'What do you make of these?' asked Jeb indicating some faint markings on the map.

Wade studied them carefully. 'They are hard to make out,' replied Wade, 'but I would say that this is supposed to be a circle and probably represents this bowl, an' these other marks seem to be pointing at the far side.'

'C'm on then let's take a closer look,' said Jeb.

The two men scrambled down the slope and crossed the rocky bowl until they were close against the massive wall of rock. They examined it carefully but could see nothing that looked as if it had once been a mine of any sort.

'There's nothing here,' said Wade dejectedly. 'Guess we followed a false trail.'

Jeb rubbed his bearded chin thoughtfully. 'What exactly are you lookin' fer, son?' he asked.

Wade was a little taken aback by this question and he looked at Jeb curiously. 'Wal, I guess I'm looking for some sort of deep shaft.'

'Thet's jest it,' answered Jeb. 'I reckon maybe we are lookin' fer the wrong thing. I know it's known as the lost mine of Superstition Mountain but maybe it isn't a mine in thet sense. It could be a hollow or merely a crack which is workable. You look to the right an' I'll go to the left but we won't be able to spend long; it will soon be gettin' dark.'

Wade moved away and the two men examined the rock face carefully. Suddenly Wade let out a yell and Jeb came running to his side. Wade had climbed a slight rise and below him he saw a slit about the height of a man cut down at an angle of forty-five degrees under the cliff-face. The two men hurried forward and started to pick their way carefully down the cutting.

'A pity we didn't bring a lantern,' said Jeb. 'We'll hev to come back tomorrow.'

'Hold it a minute,' answered Wade. 'I've got some matches here, we'll jest hev a quick look.'

He struck a match and held it above his head. The two men strained their eyes but all they saw were weird shadows cast by the flickering light. They moved a few yards further into the cutting and when Wade struck a second match they saw they were close to a wall of rock which formed the end of the slit. Suddenly Jeb gasped and moved the two yards so that he was close up to the rock.

'Bring the light near, Wade,' he said. His voice was shaking with excitement. Wade stepped forward. 'Look at this,' cried Jeb. 'We've found it!' He turned to Wade excitedly and saw the young cowboy, his eyes wide, staring incredulously at the first gold vein he had ever seen.

Suddenly he started as the match burnt his fingers. The remaining portion fell and the light went out. Wade fumbled for the matches again and his hands were shaking as he struck another match. The light flared and then burnt steadily. They examined the vein, running their fingers along it quickly.

'This sure is a bonanza,' said Jeb eagerly.

'It's here for the pickin'. It'll present no difficulty tomorrow. C'm on let's go, thet match is about done.'

Wade did not move and Jeb pulled at his arm and as the match spluttered and went out the old man turned him away from the rock. With the light ahead of them they were able to make their way out of the slit quickly.

Once they reached the bowl they stopped to get their breath. Jeb, smiling, turned to face his young companion. The smile vanished in a flash at what he saw. Wade, his fists clenched tightly so that the whites of his knuckles showed, was standing stiffly, his body tensed in excitement. His eyes were wide, a fire of unhealthy stimulation in them, as they stared at Jeb unseeingly. Suddenly he flung an arm out pointing at the cutting.

'It's there, it's all there!' Wade's voice was scarcely above a whisper but there was a tenseness in it which frightened Jeb. 'Gold! By the ton!' His eyes focused on the old man. They gleamed with an excited frenzy. 'Jeb, we're rich! We've made it! It's all ours!' The pitch of his voice rose, echoing round the bowl, thrown back in an eerie repetition.

Jeb stared at him, then suddenly his arm flashed out; his hand slashed Wade across the face like a whip. The cowboy staggered but kept his feet. He turned on Jeb, crouching like some wild animal, hatred flowing from his eyes. His Colt leaped into his hand but Jeb did not try to draw against him.

'Hold it!' rapped the old prospector. His voice cut into Wade's brain like a knife. 'Put thet away; you don't know what you're saying.'

The delayed shock of the blow suddenly penetrated into Wade's taut mind. His eyes cleared; his body relaxed. He looked down at the gun in his hand, then back to Jeb. Slowly he slipped the Colt into its holster.

'I'm sorry, Jeb,' he mumbled. 'I didn't know what I was doing.'

'Thet's all right, son,' replied the old man kindly. 'I've seen gold fever before, an' what it can do to a man. Thet's a very rich vein and your first sight of one; I hed to take drastic action; there's no tellin' what you might hev done. I've seen men kill their friends when the gold fever's been upon them. C'm on we'd better git back to camp.'

The two men retraced their steps quickly and once they reached their camp they soon had a meal ready and fell to discussing the mine.

'How much do you reckon we should take out?' asked Wade.

'Wal, I reckon if we fill the saddlebags an' our packs we'll hev plenty,' answered Jeb.

'All I want is sufficient to help the Cordobas,' said Wade. 'I'm not interested fer myself. Of course you must hev your share,' he added smiling at the old man. 'You deserve to live in comfort fer the rest of your life.'

Jeb Carter smiled thoughtfully. 'I'm not worried about riches,' he said, 'as long as I can put myself right with the people of Ascension. The thrill of finding this lost mine has been sufficient fer me.'

'Wal, we'll see what *Señor* Cordoba has to say to that,' said Wade. 'To tell you the truth I won't be sorry to git away from here; we'll make an early start in the morning. I still have a feeling those poor, unfortunate Indians turned to stone are still watching over the place.'

Jeb nodded. 'I agree,' he said. 'This mountain hasn't got its name fer nothing. Even when we get off this lump of rock we've got the desert to contend with an' we'll hev to watch out fer the Apaches.'

Although the day had been tiring neither man seemed keen for sleep and they talked far into the night. Even when they had rolled themselves in their blankets Wade found sleep did not come easily. Conchita kept coming into his mind and he kept planning what he would say to her when he returned to El Rancho Sierra de Espuma. Eventually when he dozed off he slept so soundly that he did not wake until Jeb shook him by the shoulder.

The old man had breakfast ready and after the meal they packed everything so that they could move off as soon as they returned from the mine. Armed with picks and a lantern the two men made their way to the slit on the edge of the bowl deep in the mountain. Lighting the lantern Wade led the way to the vein and the two men worked steadily until they had filled the saddle-bags and their packs.

'Wal, I guess that will do,' panted Wade as he put the last nugget into one of the bags. 'It seems a pity to leave it when there is so much more to be had.'

'Steady, son,' said Jeb wiping the sweat from his brow.

Wade laughed. 'It's all right, the fever isn't coming on again.'

They gathered up their things and retraced their steps. It was a hard journey carrying the gold and both men were relieved when they reached camp. They had just laid their packs

down and were reaching for their canteens
when they heard a boot scraping across the
rock behind them. Swinging round they
gasped with amazement when they saw
Saunders and Corby moving towards them
down the side of the hollow.

'You!' gasped Wade.

'Yeah!' laughed Saunders. 'Surprised?
Keep your hands off thet!' he snapped as
Wade moved his hand towards his gun.
'This Colt's rarin' to put a bullet in you.'

'How long you been tailin' us?' asked Jeb,
hoping they did not know of the cutting
leading to the mine.

'After we left the Apaches,' replied Saunders, 'we were lucky to meet up with some
folks. We spun them a yarn an' they fitted us
up with horses an' guns. We headed straight
fer Superstition Mountain; watched you
arrive an' hev hed our eyes on you ever since.'
He saw Jeb frown. 'We know of the entrance
to the mine,' he added with a grin, 'but
figured you may as well do the hard work fer
us, an' if thet little lot isn't enough we can
return some other time.'

'Quit talkin',' snapped Corby impatiently.
'Let's git this over an' git off this God
forsaken mountain, it gives me the creeps.'

'You've too much imagination,' laughed

Saunders. 'However, git their guns.'

Corby moved forward but in his eagerness to finish the job he stumbled over some rocks. Momentarily Saunders took his eye off Wade and Carter as his friend fell. Wade seized his chance. His hand moved like lightning to his holster and, with one movement, he drew his gun and fired it the same time diving to his left. The bullet struck Saunders in the chest sending him staggering backwards as his finger squeezed the trigger. His Colt roared but his aim had been spoiled and the lead whined harmlessly past. Wade fired again and his shot sent Saunders crashing to the ground in a silent heap. Jeb had not been slow to take the opportunity offered to him. When Corby stumbled and he saw Wade's Colt spring to life Jeb stepped sideways, quickly drawing his own gun. His finger squeezed the trigger and the bullet hit Corby between the eyes as he tried to regain his balance. With smoking Colts still in their hands the two men moved warily towards the bodies.

'The gold of Superstition Mountain still takes men to their deaths,' mused Jeb gazing at the dead men as he holstered his gun. 'Git the spades, I reckon we can find a place at the top of this hollow.'

When the shallow graves were dug and the bodies buried Wade and Jeb piled a few stones on top of them. They turned to return to their horses but froze in their tracks as two Indians with rifles covering them, emerged from behind a huge boulder.

'Drop those spades,' ordered Running Dog. 'Come forward with hands up.'

The two men did as they were told and walked slowly towards the Apaches. Wade felt an eeriness in the silence which was broken only by the scrape of their boots on the rock. The dark, cruel faces of the Indians seemed to bore into him and from this hollow the sheer rise of the cliffs felt overpowering.

'So Running Dog picked up our trail,' said Jeb as they neared the Indians.

'There was no need to trail you,' answered Running Dog coldly. 'I heard you tell Neva of the gold and knowing you would come I and Swift Bullet came and watched.'

'You know about the mine!' gasped Jeb.

A faint smile flickered across the Indian's face. 'I know,' he said. 'Running Dog will now be powerful among the Apaches. Running Dog will be able to talk to white men on equal terms. Running Dog great chief.'

'Chief?' said Jeb. 'What about Neva?'

'Neva banished,' replied the Indian

triumphantly. 'Tribe not want him after white man escape.'

Wade glanced at Jeb and felt remorse that Neva should have suffered indignities because of him.

'Not Neva's fault,' he said. 'Neva great chief. He would...'

'Neva weak, Neva fool,' spat Running Dog contemptuously. 'Neva not use knowledge of mine to bring Apache glory but now Running Dog will do that.' He turned to Swift Bullet and in answer to his order Swift Bullet moved carefully behind the white men and removed their Colts.

He was about to bind Wade's hands behind his back when a voice boomed so loudly that it seemed to come from inside the cliffs which towered over them.

'Red man, you have failed us!'

The four were startled, almost shocked by the words. Swift Bullet stopped in his movement, his face showing abject terror. Running Dog recovered almost immediately from the sudden shock and did not waver his rifle from his prisoners. Whilst keeping careful watch on Jeb and Wade he glanced at the cliffs with a mixture of curiosity and apprehension. The white men were so surprised they stood stock-still and gazed at the cliffs in amazement. Running Dog moved round the two men slowly until he had them between himself and the cliffs so that he could watch both at the same time. The voice boomed again repeating its statement.

'Who are you that call us failures?' Although Running Dog yelled at the top of his voice it sounded feeble compared with that which came from the cliffs.

'I am the ghost of the leader of the Indians turned to stone,' came the reply. 'The ghosts of my followers have languished in pain crying for release from their solitude. We are not like the ghosts of your ancestors who can ride into battle with you. It needed an Indian of noble ideals to release us so that we could accompany him to the land of the living and ride once more unseen with our fellowmen. But you have desecrated our abode. You come with no thought of us but only of yourselves; your greed for gold and power has led you along the wrong trail.'

Swift Bullet had sunk to his knees, shaking with fear. 'I told you this was an evil place,' he cried at Running Dog. 'We should never have come here.'

'Shut up,' snapped Running Dog angrily. 'But we will make the Indian great amongst white men,' he shouted towards the cliffs.

'Gold will put us on equal terms, no longer will the Red Man be looked down upon.'

'Once they know you have gold,' boomed the voice, 'they will find out where it comes from and this mountain will be reviled by them and torn to pieces. The white man will invade the land and the Indian will have to move again. Our home will be desecrated again and again just as you are desecrating it.'

'But I will show you that I mean you no harm...' started Running Dog.

'Enough!' interrupted the voice. 'You have already gone too far. It is time for you all to die.'

'Wait! Wait!' The urgent cry came faintly from under the steep cliff side. 'Do not kill these men.'

'Who are you to question me?' cried the voice.

'I am Neva, rightful chief of my tribe,' came the answer. 'I come not to seek gold but to stop Running Dog taking it and ruining my people.'

The four men in the hollow were equally surprised by the turn of events. Jeb and Wade saw a hope for their lives. Swift Bullet saw the chance of reprieve from the spirits but Running Dog's face darkened with anger when he saw himself being thwarted of the power he had gained.

'I have heard of you, Neva, you are great amongst your people,' answered the voice. 'An Indian such as you could release us from our chains.'

'My intentions are honourable,' insisted Neva. 'Because that is so, you can ride with me but first grant me the lives of these people.'

There was a moment's pause before the answer came. 'They should die but your wish is small price to pay for our freedom to ride with the living again.'

'Thank you, great one,' answered Neva.

Running Dog kept his gun trained on the two white men. 'Neva will die with you,' he hissed venomously. 'I am not afraid of these ghosts.'

'But Neva has saved our lives,' moaned Swift Bullet, 'do not throw them away again.'

At that moment a figure appeared on the edge of the hollow. Neva stopped and drew himself majestically to his full height so that he seemed to tower over the men below. Running Dog snarled and swung his rifle round quickly but Wade who had been expecting such a move flung himself at the Indian. Both men crashed on the hard rock and the rifle flew from the Apache's grasp.

Swift as lightning Running Dog leaped to his feet, pulled a knife from his belt and crouched ready to leap at Wade but a rifle crashed and a bullet spanged the rocks at his feet. The Indian froze where he was.

'Don't move, Running Dog,' shouted Neva. 'You are going to die but not that way.'

No one moved as Neva walked towards them. Swift Bullet was still on his knees but his eyes shone with admiration for his chief who had talked with the ghosts and saved his life. Wade climbed to his feet and both he and Jeb watched Neva stop in front of Running Dog whose hatred showed in his face.

Suddenly Neva handed his rifle to Jeb and pulled out a knife.

'It is you or I, Running Dog,' he said quietly.

A light came into the dark eyes of Running Dog then suddenly without warning he lunged at Neva but his chief was too quick, he side-stepped and slashed with his knife opening a small cut on Running Dog's arm. Running Dog spun round snarling with fury and hate. He leaped again but Neva repeated the manoeuvre. The two men crouched, circling round, each looking for an opening. Neva was prepared to play a waiting game and was content with nicking

Running Dog each time he made a lunge. This only helped to infuriate the Apache but underneath his brain was ice cold and in their circling he had noticed a rut which ran across the hollow. He gradually worked the unsuspecting Neva back towards it. Suddenly Neva's foot slipped in the rut; he lost his balance and fell backwards. With a yell of triumph Running Dog flung himself forward. He drew his right arm backwards and as he dropped plunged it downwards with all the force of his hatred and fury.

Neva, seeing the body and blade plummeting down on him twisted his body to the right. Running Dog's knife hit the rock with such force that it was bent and shattered in a grinding crash. Almost at the same time a piercing, frightened cry shrieked around the hollow only to be cut short. Unable to stop himself Running Dog saw that as Neva twisted he left his right arm extended with the knife blade pointing upwards!

Wade and Jeb ran forward and when Neva released his grip on the knife they pulled Running Dog's body off Neva's arm.

'Are you all right?' asked Jeb as Neva pushed himself to his feet.

The Indian nodded. 'Life is good to Neva,' he said quietly. He turned to Swift Bullet.

'My pony is close to the cliff, fetch it,' he ordered. 'You heard your chief speak with the ghosts, remember it, tell our people of Neva's doings this day and forget you ever heard of gold in this mountain. Fail to do this and Superstition Mountain will claim another victim as it has claimed three today.'

'My mind forgets already, great one,' replied Swift Bullet.

When the Indian hurried away Jeb turned to Neva. 'What went on back there?' he asked, nodding towards the cliff.

Neva smiled. 'I knew of a place called Echo Canyon, it is really only a slit in the rock but you heard the effect of my voice. I only had to take a couple of steps to one side and I became Neva talking to the ghost.'

Wade stepped forward. 'Thanks for what you did,' he said, 'when all I deserve is punishment for the trouble I brought you by rescuing your prisoners.'

Neva looked hard at Wade. 'That was wrong of you to break your word – too many white men have done that to the Indians – but I think I would do the same if you held some of my people captive. And I do not forget you save my life just now, nor that you want the gold only for *Señor* Cordoba. Come I will take you back to my village and see you safely out of the troubled country.'

Three days later Neva led Jeb and Wade into the Indian encampment. Swift Bullet had prevailed upon his chief to allow him to go on ahead and prepare the Apaches for his arrival.

'You trust him after he sided with Running Dog?' asked Jeb surprised at the chief's faith in this man.

'There is no deep harm in Swift Bullet,' replied Neva. 'He is easily led and Running Dog, knowing this, sought an ally. The ghost of Superstition Mountain left its mark on Swift Bullet.'

There was great rejoicing when the three men entered the camp. Swift Bullet had lost no time in claiming Neva their rightful chief and in telling the Apaches how he could talk on equal terms with the ghosts of the Indians turned to stone; how he had saved the Pima ghosts from everlasting imprisonment on Superstition Mountain, how Neva had fought Running Dog and defeated him and how he would make the Apaches great again. The Indians had listened eagerly to his story and prepared a great welcome for their chief.

Neva persuaded Jeb and Wade to rest in the camp for a few days but on the evening of the second day Jeb, sensing that Wade was impatient to be going, told Neva they would be leaving the following morning.

'Wade wishes to put things right with the Cordobas,' he explained.

'Give my greetings to *Señor* Cordoba,' said Neva. 'Tell him we are grateful that he kept the secret of the mine.'

Wade looked hard at the chief. 'Neva,' he said. 'That secret will remain with us too. No white man will invade your land because of us. We will not betray your trust.' He looked sadly at the fire. 'I did once, Neva, and for that I am ashamed, you are worth more than all those white men whom I released.'

'That is finished,' answered the Apache. 'Neva thinks of it no more. He knows you for the good in you.'

Wade smiled. 'Thank you, Neva,' he said, his voice full of emotion. He pulled the map from his pocket. 'As long as this map exists there is danger that it might be stolen and that could mean great trouble for your people. I think *Señor* Cordoba would approve of my action.' He pushed himself to his feet, strode close to the fire and threw the paper into the flame. Red man and white man watched the fire devour the key to the lost mine of Superstition Mountain.

FIFTEEN

Manuel Cordoba sat in his chair on the veranda of his ranch-house and gazed along his beloved valley. He had not been well of late and he feared he might die leaving the troubles caused by drought and money shortage to his grandchildren whereas he had dreamed of leaving them in fortunate circumstances. He wondered if he had used his share of the gold as well as he might; should he not have spent so much trying to find his brother?

His thoughts were interrupted by the rustle of skirts behind him. Conchita laid her hand on his shoulder as she passed behind him and came to sit down at his feet.

'Worrying again, grandfather?' she said softly.

'I am sorry, Conchita, I should not let you see it,' he answered. 'You have worries of your own. You have not been the same since Wade O'Hara rode out of here with your heart.'

Conchita stiffened. 'He did not take my

heart,' she said coldly. 'I am angry that he deceived me, and that he hurt you. If he had not stolen that map you would have had no worries now because you could have got more gold from the mine.'

'I would not have done that,' replied Manuel firmly. 'That mountain is evil and I would have sacrificed no one of mine to it. When I tried to stop Wade from going I was not interested in recovering the map for the map's sake but for two reasons. I did not want Wade to combat the mountain and I gave my word to the Apaches that I would keep the secret of the mine otherwise white men would have swarmed all over their country. Now if that map gets into the wrong hands...'

'It is already in the wrong hands,' snapped Conchita. 'You seem to think Wade will guard the secret.'

'I think he might, Conchita,' answered Manuel. 'On reflection I think there might be some truth in his story, after all we liked him.'

'He deceived us,' hissed Conchita. 'If he were here now I would kill him.'

'Then you may have your wish,' said the old man gently, 'for if I'm not mistaken he is coming along the valley.' The announcement was made so calmly that for a moment the meaning of the words did not register in Conchita's mind. Then suddenly she sat upright.

'What!' she gasped.

Manuel pointed to two horsemen in the distance. 'The one on the right sits a horse like Wade O'Hara,' he observed. Conchita jumped to her feet but before she could move into the house her grandfather grabbed her by the arm. 'See he rides with only one companion, a small man, and neither Saunders nor Corby were small.'

Conchita turned round slowly and stood silently beside her grandfather watching the two riders grow bigger as they rode towards them.

Her face was impassive and Manuel did not speak as Wade and Jeb pulled their horses to a stop in front of the house and swung from the saddle.

'*Señor* Cordoba,' said Wade. 'I know I may not be welcome here but I had to come to keep my promise.' He paused searching for words. Manuel smiled and nodded but Conchita stared straight ahead. 'May I present Jeb Carter,' continued Wade. 'He helped me as you already know and I shared the secret of Superstition Mountain with him but it is a secret in a safe place, Jeb will not reveal it to anyone.'

'And what about you, and your other two friends, can we trust you to keep it?' snapped Conchita suddenly coming to life. Her eyes were wild with fire and the words flew from her mouth like the fangs of a snake.

'Conchita,' said Wade, 'I know I behaved badly but it was necessary. Saunders and Corby are dead but please hear my story.' Wade hesitated looking hard at the girl but she did not answer.

'Carry on, my son,' said Manuel. 'We will listen.'

Wade told them everything from the moment he had ridden from El Rancho Sierra de Espuma. They listened in silence and when he had finished the old man nodded. 'You did well, Wade, to beat the mountain, you see how the mountain still spreads its evil through death.'

'And the map?' asked Conchita. 'I expect that will be used again?'

'The map is no more,' replied Jeb. 'Wade burnt it before we left the Indians. He knew of the agreement your grandfather had made with them and he was prepared to do the same.'

'I will not return to the mountain,' said

Wade. 'I took all the gold I wanted.' As he spoke he and Jeb moved to the pack horse and removed the bags from its back. They walked to the veranda and laid them in front of Manuel. 'All the gold I wanted,' repeated Wade, 'is there, to help put this ranch in a strong position again.'

Manuel and Conchita stared at the bags and then at Wade. Conchita suddenly burst out crying, spun on her heels and ran into the house.

'Thank you, son,' said the old man. 'I knew there was good in you. Conchita doubted you, now she is ashamed.'

'There is nothing for her to be ashamed of,' said Wade. 'I deserved all she thought of me.'

'Go to her, son,' said Manuel. 'Jeb and I will discuss how best to make amends with his friends in Ascension but one thing is certain, you will both remain here and share in my ranch.'

Wade mumbled his thanks and crossed the veranda quickly.

'Tell Conchita to plan to have the wedding soon,' shouted Manuel as Wade was closing the ranchhouse door behind him.